A TIME TO KILL

When the law no longer protects you

RION CARPADAKIS

CHAPTER 1

THE SHOOTING

It's sunny and clear on the morning of March 16th. It's cold outside, but no snow is on the ground. Al's Diner is filled with locals enjoying their breakfasts. Judy Baker, one of the waitresses on duty, is going about her normal routine.

A police car pulls into the parking lot. Officer Mike Murphy parks, gets out of his car, and comes into the diner for breakfast, something he does regularly. Most mornings he'd sit with other officers, but today he wants to be alone. Judy sees him come in and greets him, then shows him to a booth next to a window overlooking his patrol car.

Once he's seated, she says, "Hey, Mike. How are you? Would you like some coffee this morning?"

"Yes. Thanks, Judy," he says.

"No problem. Are you going to have the usual?" she asks.

"Actually, I think I'm going to look over the menu and maybe try something new today," Mike says.

Judy hands him a menu, then leaves to take another order. He enjoys his coffee, watching the local weather on TV until she returns. Soon after taking his order, Judy returns with Mike's breakfast, and he returns to watching the news.

As he is eating, a black sedan, driven by Robert Land, pulls into the parking lot of the diner. After seeing Mike's car in the parking lot and noticing him through the window, Robert pulls out his cell phone and makes a call.

"Hello?"

"I've found him, sir," Robert says.

"Where are you?"

"I'm at Al's Diner."

"OK, I'll be there in 10 minutes."

Robert ends the call and waits.

About ten minutes later, another black sedan pulls into the parking lot and parks next to Robert, then a middle-aged man gets out of the car. Robert and the man come face to face as Robert pulls out an automatic handgun from his coat pocket and hands it to the man.

"Thank you, Robert. Now, I think it's time for you to leave," he says.

"Sir, are you sure you really want to do this?" Robert asks.

"Yes, Robert. You know I have to do this. I want you to follow the instructions I've given you, okay?"

"Yes, sir. I understand. I'll take care of it. Good luck, sir."

Both men stare at each other with sad expressions as they ponder what's about to happen, taking a moment to reflect on their friendship. Robert wishes the man good luck, then both men embrace. Judy takes notice of the exchange from inside the diner, then watches as Robert gets back into his car and drives off down the road.

The other man puts the gun in his coat pocket and walks towards the diner, glancing at the patrol car along the way, determined to carry out his plan.

As he enters the diner, Judy is delivering an order at the other end of the restaurant. Several booths from the door, Mike is finishing his breakfast and reading a newspaper, never noticing the man walk in. Not waiting to be seated, the man walks slowly down the aisle towards Mike. As he approaches, Mike looks up from the newspaper, staring at the man with surprise and fear in his eyes as the man stops about 5 feet in front of him.

The man pulls the handgun out of his coat pocket and quickly lifts it up, pointing it directly at Mike. Having delivered her order, Judy turns towards the front of the restaurant and sees the man aiming his gun at Mike, who tries unsuccessfully to pull his service pistol out of its holster as the man starts shooting.

The first shot hits Mike in the center of his forehead, killing him instantly. Debris splatters everywhere as the back of his head is blown off. Judy and several customers start screaming, some taking cover under tables. The gunman fires the remainder of his bullets, shooting into Mike's chest and face, making him unrecognizable. Finally, Mike falls to the floor, dead, with pieces of him left at the table.

As he turns to leave the diner, the gunman looks at Judy. At the door, he stops before exiting to observe the mess and dead officer. The customers look on as the man says clearly to Mike's dead body,

"You will never hurt another person again." He then walks out to his black sedan and drives off.

A quick-thinking customer had called 911 after the first shot, so within minutes several police cars swarm into the parking lot. Officers exit their cars and run into the diner with guns drawn, unsure if the gunman is still inside. They see the dead officer in a pool of blood. Some customers, too afraid to come out, are still hiding under tables and behind the counter. Officer Mark Smith, the first to enter the diner, approaches Mike's body after Judy tells them the gunman just left. Shocked by the gruesome scene, Mark asks if anyone saw which way the suspect went.

Amy Silvers, a young patron who was seated a few tables away from Mike, responds. "He was a white man. He looked like he was maybe between forty and fifty. He drove off in a black car that way--"

She points in the direction in which the man drove off, and several officers race out of the diner in search of the gunman. Mark then asks if anyone needs medical attention. When no one responds, he calls the dispatcher to give a description of the suspect and car.

Another officer walks up to Mike's body and turns him onto his back, searching his pockets for anything that might identify him. His eyes widen as he realizes the identity of the dead man.

"Jesus Christ! This is Officer Mike Murphy!"

CHAPTER 2

POLICE RESPONSE

Mark questions Amy and Judy, asking if they can give a description of the gunman. Directly behind Mark, the TV is showing a news story, and Amy has a look of shock on her face when she sees the gunman on the screen in a story unrelated to the shooting.

"That's him!" she exclaims.

Mark and the other officer look up in disbelief at the TV in the middle of a news story about local billionaire Phillip Bates. He asks Amy, "This man? Phillip Bates? Are you sure that's the man who did this?"

Amy confirms he is the man who killed the police officer. With his radio, Mark updates headquarters, telling the dispatcher the suspect has been identified as Phillip Bates. The dispatcher is caught off guard and asks Mark to confirm that he's referring to Phillip Bates.

"Phillip Bates? You mean that rich guy? The billionaire?" she asks.

"Yes, billionaire Phillip Bates is the suspect. We're going to need homicide and paramedics out here immediately," he responds, then resumes questioning Amy. "Amy, can you give me a little bit more information? Tell me exactly what happened, what you saw and heard."

"Yeah. The guy came in, walked up to the police officer, and just started shooting," she says.

"Did the suspect say anything to anyone or threaten anyone else after shooting the officer?"

"Yes, actually, right before he left, he looked at the man and said, 'You will never hurt another person again.'"

"You will never hut another person again? Did it look like these men knew each other?"

"I don't know. I couldn't see the officer's face because I was sitting in a booth behind him. I was facing the man when he was shooting and wasn't even looking at them until he started shooting."

"Did you notice anyone else with him? Or could you tell if there was anyone in the car with him before he came in?"

"No, he was alone when he came in, but I didn't see him in the parking lot before he got here, since I was eating breakfast with my dad."

Judy suddenly interrupts Amy to tell Mark she'd seen him in the parking lot before he entered the diner. "The suspect was talking to another man in the parking lot, and he and the other man hugged each other before the other man left," she says.

"Hugged each other? Can you describe the other man or the car he was driving?" Mark asks.

"It was just a big, black car, not sure what kind. Some kind of big sedan. It looked like maybe a Cadillac, but it was too hard to tell."

Mark stands and tells all the patrons of the diner he'll need statements from each of them about what they saw before they can leave the scene.

* * *

The parking lot of the diner has been taped off with crime scene tape, and onlookers are looking at the scene from the curb on the other side of the road. Homicide supervisor Alex Caldwell gets out of his car in the parking lot and goes into the diner. As he enters, Mark approaches him, having just finished interviewing the customers who witnessed the shooting.

"Hey, Alex, how's it going?" Mark says.

"Hey, Mark. What have you got here?"

"Well, from what we've gotten so far, it looks like Phillip Bates walked in, pulled out a handgun, killed officer Mike Murphy, then drove off in a big black car, possibly a Cadillac. We've got several witnesses who have identified Phillip Bates as the suspect. They say he walked right up to the officer without any warning and just opened fire. He emptied the entire magazine into Mike before leaving. One of the witnesses here also said right after he killed Mike, he said, 'You'll never hurt another person again.' Apparently, he was after Mike only."

Alex looks around the diner and notices two security cameras on the roof in two different corners of the diner. He then asks Judy, "Do those security cameras work?"

She says, "Yes, they work."

"OK, I need to see the video from both the cameras. Where's the video machine?"

"It's back in the office."

Judy escorts Alex and Mark to the back office, where the security recording machine is located. The video monitor is a split screen, showing the view from both cameras at the same time. Judy plays back the video as Mark and Alex both watch. The video and audio clearly show Phillip Bates come in and kill the officer. Even though Alex has been in homicide for years, he's shocked at the video and surprised to know Phillip Bates, a well-respected businessman, is the gunman.

"Jesus…that really is Phillip Bates," Mark says.

Alex responds, "He looks like a man on a mission to me. Looks like Mike was his sole target. Maybe a revenge killing."

"I agree. He went right for Mike. Mike never had a chance. Look at the time. Phillip was in and out in less than a minute!"

After they review the video several times, Mark takes the DVD of the video from Judy and drops it into a plastic evidence bag. Judy, Alex, and Mark then leave the office and return to the front of the diner, where detectives are still collecting evidence, getting fingerprints, interviewing witnesses, and photographing the scene. Other officers on the scene are talking to each other, discussing the case. One officer sarcastically says the killing couldn't have happened to a nicer person. The other officer agrees.

It's apparent – at least between these two officers – Mike Murphy wasn't a well-liked officer.

* * *

At the station, the police chief, Dan Brady, is about to hold a meeting with the entire department to update everyone on the case. The briefing room is full, including Mayor Steve Wilson.

The chief walks up to the podium. "All right, guys, listen up. As you've heard by now, Officer Mike Murphy was gunned down this morning at Al's Diner. We have surveillance video and positive ID from several witnesses identifying Phillip Bates as the suspect. We've just issued a warrant for his arrest for the murder. I've just gotten off the phone with Mr. Bates's attorney. He hasn't heard from him and doesn't know where he is.

Now look, for those of you who don't know the full background of Phillip Bates, he's a very well-known, well-respected person in the community. A multi-billionaire, considered a hero by many. He's donated and spent millions of dollars helping people for years through his foundation. He builds schools, hospitals, homeless shelters, and animal shelters. He's the state's largest employer through his various companies. I know he even employs some of you in your off hours. His foundation had just recently paid for the community Christmas Day dinner and annual Tree Lighting Ceremony, where he announced the construction of Bates Community College I, myself, have had a lot of respect for this man.

At the same time, as you're also aware from recent events, Officer Mike Murphy has been involved in a lot of controversy lately. He was involved in an investigation into the shooting death of an African American teenager who he claimed pointed a firearm at him. This incident has resulted in recent protests in the city.

Now, I realize many of you may have been friends with Mike, but I want to make perfectly clear: This arrest is going to be done by the book. The media is all over this story. There's a lot of publicity here. The public isn't going to be happy about this man being arrested and charged, no matter what he's done. I won't tolerate any overly aggressive tactics or revenge against this man. He's innocent until proven guilty in a court of law. I don't need to have another riot start in my city because one of my officers decides to get out of line. I hope I've made myself clear. Now, Mayor Wilson would like to make a brief statement."

Mayor Wilson walks up to the podium to make his statement.

"Good morning. I have a brief statement. I just want to clarify that I am in full agreement with Chief Brady that this arrest must be done by the book. This city does a lot of business with Phillip Bates and he has been a very well-respected member of the community for a long time. So please, let's keep it professional okay? Thank You."

Dan Brady walks back up to the podium and says "Thank You Mr. Mayor. Let's get this done, people. That is all."

As Brady finishes his briefing, officers leave the room, heading to their cars.

CHAPTER 3

THE SEARCH FOR A KILLER

Phillip Bates knew what he was going to do. He realized the police would be hunting for him after the killing, and he didn't want the front gate of his estate destroyed by police cars ramming through it. So, he left the gate to his residence open so officers could drive onto the property; however, they'd be quite surprised when they got there.

Police cars swarm into the driveway of Phillip Bates's house. Once parked, the officers take up positions behind their cars, with guns pointed at the front of the residence, not knowing what to expect.

Police Supervisor Martin Wells pulls a bullhorn out of his car and starts speaking. "Phillip Bates, this is Officer Martin Wells, of the Metro Police. You are ordered to come out with your hands in the air. The house is completely surrounded. You will not be harmed if you surrender immediately."

Media trucks pull up just outside the gates of the property to film what's happening. After no response comes from the house for a few moments, Martin shouts again through the bullhorn.

"Phillip Bates, this is your last warning. You are ordered to surrender immediately. Come out with your hands in the air."

Again, no response.

Martin then orders the other officers to move in slowly. As they do, they keep their weapons trained on the front door. As they get about halfway to it, the door opens. The officers stop and prepare to open fire as an older man exits the home, hands in the air. It's clear he's the butler from his appearance. He is wearing a dark black uniform that looks like the kind of uniform a butler would wear.

Martin says, "Freeze! Keep your hands in the air and turn around." The butler does as instructed. "Start walking backwards slowly." The butler follows the instructions as the officers keep their weapons aimed at him. When he gets about 10 feet from the officers, Martin says, "Stop. Get down on your knees."

The butler gets down on his knees as the officers behind him, including Martin, approach. Martin asks him his name. Nervous, the butler stutters a bit while identifying himself.

"Uhh…my name is George, sir. I'm one of the house staff," he says.

"Is there anyone else inside the house?" Martin asks.

"No, sir, I'm the only one home."

The officers make sure the butler isn't armed before telling him he can get up so they can talk to him.

Martin then asks, "Where's your boss? Where's Phillip Bates?"

George responds, "I don't know. He left about 3 hours ago. He said he was going to meet with his attorney. Before he left, he gave me instructions to leave the front gate open, and if anyone should come here looking for him, I'm supposed to give you this." He hands the officer a business card for Phillip Bates's attorney, Paul Goodwin.

"We have a warrant to search the premises," Martin tells George as he hands him the warrant.

Several officers then enter the premises to search for Phillip and any possible evidence.

* * *

In the midst of the entire city's massive manhunt for Phillip after Mike's killing, Phillip has come to his attorney's office.

Paul Goodwin is a middle-aged white man, slightly balding and a little overweight. He is the kind of person who loves using his hands when he talks. He and Phillip have been very good friends for years, and he's been Phillip's attorney for several years as well.

After Phillip explains, in explicit detail, what he's done, Paul gets on the phone and calls the police department. He asks to speak to the police chief regarding the surrender of Phillip Bates and tells the operator he's Bates's attorney. The operator immediately connects him to Brady.

Paul then tells Brady Phillip has contacted him and wishes to turn himself in and wants assurances that Phillip won't be harmed when he comes to the police station. Brady gives his personal assurance that Phillip will be safe and explains to Paul what'll happen to Phillip upon his surrender. Paul tells the chief he understands and they'll be down within the hour. He then ends the call and turns to Phillip.

"OK, I just got off the phone with Dan Brady. He said you'll be safe. You'll be placed under arrest and booked into the jail and segregated from other inmates. You'll then be brought in front of a judge within a couple hours to hear charges. The judge will decide on bail at that point. I'm guessing bail will be unlikely in your case because of the publicity and given the fact that the victim was a police officer.

"You know, Phillip, I have to ask. With all the resources at your disposal, why didn't you just hire someone else to whack this guy? Why did you do this yourself? And why, for God's sake, in a crowded restaurant full of witnesses and security cameras recording the whole thing?"

Phillip responds, "Paul, after everything this officer's done, there was no way I was going to allow him to hurt anyone else again. Last night was the last straw. I made myself a promise I would never allow that man to hurt anyone else again and he would pay for what he'd done. And Paul, you know I always keep my promises. I needed to do this myself."

"Yeah, you do keep your promises. I have to give you that one," Paul says. "Well, I'll do my best to get bail for you. This city wouldn't be what it is today if it wasn't for your financial support, as well as your foundation. Hopefully, the judge will take that into account."

Phillip responds, "Hopefully so. Paul, I want this trial to come as soon as possible. I don't want this to be dragged out. All the things this cop has done are still fresh in everyone's minds. I think that will work to my advantage."

Paul responds, "Yeah, you're right about that. I'll try my best Phillip. Are you ready to go get this done?"

Phillip says he's ready, then both he and Paul leave the office and get into Paul's car. Paul then drives Phillip to the police station. When they arrive, Paul pulls into the visitor parking lot, where they see several reporters waiting out in front of the entrance; they'd arrived earlier in anticipation of Phillip surrendering to the police. As Paul and Phillip head towards the station entrance, Paul tells Phillip to remain silent as they pass the reporters, that he'll handle them; nonetheless, the reporters mob them with questions.

"Phillip, why did you kill Officer Murphy?"

"Did Officer Murphy threaten you?"

"Who is currently in charge at your companies?"

Paul responds with, "No comment" to each of the reporters.

As he and Phillip enter the lobby of the police station, several reporters attempt to enter the station with them but are stopped at the door by a police officer waiting for Phillip's arrival. Several officers in the lobby see Phillip come in and just stare in disbelief and shock at the man who's just murdered one of their brothers in arms.

Paul and Phillip approach the front desk to speak to the desk sergeant "Yes, hello. My name is Paul Goodwin. I'm an attorney. I represent Mr. Phillip Bates, who is here to surrender for questioning regarding the death of Officer Mike Murphy."

The lobby is now in complete silence as several officers and other various individuals continue to stare in disbelief. The desk sergeant stands up and comes out to make the arrest personally. As he approaches Phillip, he stops in front of him and looks into his face, with guilt written all over his own; he feels sorry that he has to arrest the man everyone knows and has admired for so long.

The sergeant says, "Phillip, I'm sorry, sir, but I need you to please turn around and place your hands behind your back."

Phillip responds, "It's okay, sonny. There's nothing to be sorry about. I know you have to do your job."

Phillip turns around, and the sergeant cuffs him, reads him his rights, and asks if he's willing to talk to the police regarding the charges against him.

Phillip responds, "I will speak to you only in the presence of my attorney here."

The sergeant responds, "That's fine. Paul, I need you to wait here in the lobby while I take Phillip back and get him booked in, then you'll be brought back to join him for questioning."

The sergeant then takes Phillip into the back room for further processing.

CHAPTER 4

JEROME GOSHEN ARRESTED

3 Months Earlier – December 15th

Jerome Goshen and his girlfriend, Charlene Jones, both African American, live in a small house in town, on a residential street. The style of houses and look of the neighborhood indicate their area of town is for predominantly lower income people.

It's the middle of the day, and Jerome is home, watching TV with some of his friends. Charlene arrives home from work and walks in the front door to see him sitting in a recliner in the living room, with three of his friends sitting on the couch. All three friends are also Black. Next to the recliner where Jerome is sitting is a table with empty beer cans. A coffee table in front of the couch also has a lot of empty beer cans, as well as empty cigarette boxes and a plate with cigarette butts and ashes; it's clear Jerome and his three friends are all getting drunk.

Charlene has been working all day and is tired and just wanted to come home and relax. She's very angry to see all the beer cans all over the place and wants to know where the money for the beer came from, as neither Jerome nor any of his friends are working.

She asks Jerome, "What's going on here? Where'd y'all get the beer from?"

Jerome snaps, "Where do you think? From the store!"

Charlene tells Jerome, "Don't get smart with me. Where did you get the money for it?" While waiting for a response, she sees one of Jerome's friends smoking. "And what the hell are you doing smoking in my house?" she asks.

The friend immediately puts out the cigarette, then Charlene turns her attention back to Jerome, demanding an answer to her question about the money.

"I got the money from the bedroom!" Jerome says.

Charlene opens her eyes wide and quickly storms off into the bedroom. After a moment, she comes storming back.

"You spent our savings money on beer? That's our damn rent money!" Her anxiety levels spike as she realizes the rent money, which is due tomorrow, is now gone. "The rent is due tomorrow! What the hell were you thinking?! Where the hell is the money supposed to come from now?!" she asks.

Jerome responds, "You get paid tomorrow. Use that to pay the rent. Now leave me the hell alone."

"That paycheck is for our food and electricity, not for you to buy beer for your fucking friends!" Charlene then turns her anger on Jerome's three friends on the couch. "You all need to get the hell out right now, because shit's about to fly in here!"

Jerome's friends look at each other for a moment, then very quickly race toward the front door, showing just how scared of her they are. As the last of them approaches the door, he turns to look at Jerome and wishes him good luck. He then exits the front door as Charlene turns to face Jerome, still sitting in the recliner.

*　*　*

A few blocks away, Officers Brian Davis and Mike Murphy are sitting in their patrol car on the side of the road, talking while waiting for a radio call or speeders.

Brian asks, "Hey, did you see *The Walking Dead* last night?"

Mike responds, "No, Carol and I got into it again. She started going off, screaming her head off as usual."

Brian asks, "What was it about this time?"

Mike responds, "Ahh, same crap as usual, money and work. I'm working too much, not giving her enough attention. I swear, the bitch is driving me crazy! She's demanding shit that just isn't gonna happen. She gets pissed every time I go out with you or the guys. It's like she wants me home right after work all the time and not to have any free time to myself. It's really pissing me off, a lot."

"I'm sorry to hear that, man. I know what you're going through. Jan and I went through the same crap two years ago."

Mike asks, "Is that why you aren't married to her anymore?"

Brian responds, "Hell yeah, that's why! Neither of us could take it anymore. We both just decided it was better to split up. I mean, don't get me wrong. I missed her a lot when we first separated, but at least the fighting stopped. Now, we're better friends than when we were married. Hell, we even still get together sometimes just to fuck!"

Mike responds, "Well, the only sex I've had with Carol lately was hallway sex last night."

"You just said you were fighting…then you had sex in your hallway afterward?"

"Exactly! We were fighting, then afterward we passed each other in the hallway and she looked right at me and said, 'AHH, FUCK YOU!' That's about all the sex I've had lately!"

Davis starts laughing uncontrollably, then says, "Man, I'm sorry. That's some funny shit, dude!"

Just as Mike starts to laugh, too, a call comes over the radio.

"All units, 415 in progress. 1038 South Oak Street. Woman calling in, reporting her boyfriend is drunk and threatening her and refusing to leave. Boyfriend is described as a black male, 38 years old, approximately 250 lbs., five-ten."

Brian looks at Mike and asks, "Do you wanna take it?"

Mike responds, "Hell yeah, let's go."

Brian calls in to headquarters to report that they're responding to the call. Their car then speeds out of the parking lot towards Charlene's house.

Meanwhile, across town Charlene is standing in front of Jerome, who's still sitting in the recliner. She tells him, "I'm fuckin' done with you. I'm done supporting your fat, lazy ass. You don't do shit except sit around and watch fucking TV all day and get drunk with your friends. You don't help me out at all. You won't work, you won't help pay for shit, and you won't even try to look for a damn job — and you ain't even no good in bed neither. I'm fuckin' done with you! I want you to get the hell out. I don't love you anymore and don't want you here anymore. Just go. Take your shit and get the hell out!"

Jerome responds, "Bitch, please. You say the same shit every damn week. Why don't you just shut the hell up, before I shut you up? And go get your ass in the kitchen and make me something to eat." He then mumbles to himself, saying, "God damn, fuckin' bitch" in a low voice.

She hears him mumble this, and it sets her off. She starts screaming at him as she stands over him and can see out the window behind him to the street. Once she notices the police car with Brian and Mike pull up and sees them get out, she starts screaming even louder.

"You son of a bitch! You don't do shit here, and you're calling *me* a bitch? Get out! Get the hell out! We're done. I want your lazy ass outta here – now!"

Charlene reaches down and grabs Jerome's arm to pull him up out of the chair, knowing his temper will cause him to explode just as the police are coming up to the front door.

Just as she suspected, Jerome aggressively and quickly gets up out of the chair as she's still holding his arm and says, "God damn bitch!", then pulls her hand off his arm, holds her arm with one hand, and starts slapping her in the face with the other hand. Right as he slaps her, Officers Davis and Murphy come into view in the open front door and see Jerome slap Charlene in the face.

Mike yells out, "Hey!" and rips open the screen door. He and Brian then charge in and tackle Jerome to the floor.

Jerome starts to scream. "Get off me, man! Man, I didn't do nothing!"

Mike and Brian have Jerome pinned down, facing the floor, and force his hands behind his back. Mike then puts handcuffs on Jerome, tells him he's under arrest, then they lift him up onto his feet.

Brian calls in on the radio that they have one in custody and to cancel the request for further assistance. Jerome insists he didn't do anything and tries to put the blame on Charlene, saying she's just "trippin' out."

"I just saw you hit her in the face. You're going downtown. Brian, get him out of here," Mike says.

As Jerome's being led toward the front door, he turns to Charlene and says, "I'm sorry, baby. I'll be back soon."

Charlene responds, "Hell no. Don't 'sorry, baby' me. You aren't *ever* coming back here. Your shit will be by the front door when you get out."

Mike stays inside to question Charlene. "What's your name, ma'am?"

"My name is Charlene Jones, sir."

"OK, Charlene, can you tell me what happened here?"

"Yeah, I just got home from work and found Jerome sitting around, getting drunk with his friends. Then I found out he used all the rent money to pay for beer for his friends – and the rent's due tomorrow. Now I don't have any way to pay the rent. I told him I was done with him and he needed to get the hell out. He wouldn't go, so I grabbed his arm to pull him out of the chair, and he slapped me. That was right when you showed up."

Mike nods, indicating he understands what she's saying. "Is he on the lease here with you, ma'am?" he asks.

"No, this is my house. He has his own place, but he's been coming over almost every day. I want him gone. I don't want him coming here no more."

"OK. Well, we're going to take him downtown and book him for assault. He'll spend the night in jail, and he'll go before a judge tomorrow. Unless he has an outstanding warrant, he'll probably be out of jail tomorrow. Maybe you might consider looking for a new boyfriend."

"I don't want a boyfriend anymore. I'm done with that. All I wanted was for Jerome to leave."

Mike hands her a business card. "Well, he's out tonight. And he won't be back tonight. Here's a card. I want you to call if you need anything else. You can also find out information about Jerome's case from that number. I recommend you don't let him come back into the house again if he shows up here."

"Oh, he ain't comin' back in here again. HELL NO!"

"OK, do you want us to give him a trespass warning, letting him know he'll be arrested if he comes back here?"

"Yeah. Yeah, please do that. I don't want him here no more."

"OK. We'll give him the warning. If he shows back up here again, call 911, and we'll be back out here immediately to place him under arrest again, OK? Have a good evening, ma'am."

Mike goes out to the car, where Brian is finishing filling out a booking form for Jerome. He asks Brian, "Did you get all the info for him?"

"Yeah. I've got everything here. What did she have to say?"

"She said she came home from work to find this 'boyfriend' inside with his friends, getting drunk. And apparently, this dumb motherfucker used her rent money to buy the beer."

Brian looks surprised and says, "Oh, Jesus. Man, what a dumb shit."

Mike responds, "Yeah, he is. So, she told him to get his shit and get the fuck out and started talking trash to him and grabbed his arm to try to throw his ass out, and that's when he grabbed her arm and started slapping her around right when we got there."

Brian asks, "Are we charging her with anything?"

Mike responds, "No! This guy is a piece of shit. She asked us to give him a trespass warning. Let's just give him the warning, then book him in for assault."

Mike and Brian go to the back door of the car, then open it to give Jerome his warning. Mike says, "Jerome, we're giving you a trespass warning not to come near this house again. If you come near this house again, you'll be arrested. We're taking you downtown now, where you'll be booked for assault. You're going to spend the night in jail, then go before a judge in the morning. Do you understand?"

Jerome just looks at Mike and nods that he understands. Mike slams the car door shut in his face, then he and Brian get in the front seat to go to the station, with Brian driving.

As they're driving towards the jail, Mike starts talking to Jerome about what he did. He asks him, "So, what the fuck is wrong with you? You had a woman in there working hard, paying the bills, and you just fucked it all up for yourself. You're just sitting around, not doing shit, being a lazy motherfucker – and then you blow her rent money buying beer for your friends? Man, you're one sorry motherfucker. I would have kicked your ass out, too, ya' fuckin loser."

Jerome responds, "Man, you don't know what the fuck you're talking about. And I'll be right back over at her house tomorrow, fucking her brains out again!"

This sets Mike off, and he tells Jerome, "If you show up tomorrow night at her house, I'll be there, too. And when I get done with you, the only pussy you'll ever be able to get is the kind you have to inflate. I don't give a shit what she wants. WE gave you the trespass warning, not her. Your ass will be right back in jail if you show up at her house, you punk-ass bitch."

Jerome responds, "You ain't gonna be able to do shit. You show up tomorrow, and I'll fuck you up. You're lucky I got these handcuffs on right now, you punk-ass white honky piece of shit!"

Right when he says that, Jerome also kicks the back of Mike's seat very hard, which causes him to jolt forward. This absolutely infuriates Mike and sends him into a rage. He makes eye contact with Brian, then tells him to pull the car over to the side of the road. Brian shoots Mike a questioning look, then Mike speaks loud, firmly, and more demanding, telling him, "PULL THE CAR OVER NOW! I'm not gonna take this shit from this fucking nigger!"

Brian looks in the rear-view mirror at Jerome, tells him he just fucked up, then pulls the car over to the side of the road. Mike gets out of the car, opens the back door, and pulls out his nightstick.

As a police officer, Mike seriously crosses the line here as he loses control of himself while violently assaulting Jerome with his nightstick, yelling racially sensitive statements to him at the same time.

He hits Jerome in the head and chest with his nightstick as he screams, "You think that's funny? Huh? You think that's funny, you fuckin' nigger piece of shit?" He continues assaulting Jerome. "You're gonna threaten me and kick my seat, huh? Talk more shit now, nigger! Kick my seat again, you black piece of shit," Mike screams as he continues his assault.

Brian tells Mike, "Mike, that's enough."

But Mike just hits Jerome again, making him scream out in pain for the cop to stop.

"You fucking black piece of shit! I don't give a fuck about any of you scum bags! I fuckin' hate you niggers!" Mike screams.

"Mike, that's enough!" Brian yells.

Mike looks up at Brian and suddenly realizes he's crossed a line, then stops his assault. Jerome looks beaten to hell, with blood coming out of his nose and mouth. Mike tells Brian to help him restrain Jerome's legs, then they'll take him to the hospital. With his legs restrained, Mike and Brian get back in their car and drive off towards the hospital. Brian shoots Mike an evil look, and Mike realizes just how unhappy with him Brian is. Brian then calls in to base to report they're transporting the 415 suspect to the hospital.

As they pull up to the emergency room entrance, the hospital staff comes out to the car. Seeing Jerome's condition, they hurriedly help him out of the car and onto a gurney. Brian then removes Jerome's handcuffs from one hand and shackles him to the gurney.

Brian and Mike follow the staff inside to give them their official statement. At the counter, where a triage nurse is seated, they tell her they're bringing in the suspect, Jerome Goshen, for evaluation and treatment.

When the nurse asks what's wrong with him, Brian explains, "Uh, we had to –"

Mike suddenly interrupts him, explaining that the suspect started to fight and resist when they were attempting to arrest him and they were forced to restrain him. He says it took a little bit more force than they would have liked, but the suspect completely refused to cooperate.

The nurse asks them to fill out the necessary forms, then says it'll take about an hour for Jerome to be treated. After filling out the forms, Mike and Brian decide to go get some lunch while they wait.

On the way to the fast food place, Brian makes it clear to Mike that he seriously crossed a line when he beat Jerome. "Dude, you know that was some fucked up shit you did to that guy. You need to learn to control yourself better before you end up getting us both in a lot of trouble."

"I know," Mike says. "I'm sorry I lost it out there. I'm just so tired of these fucking niggers. They really make me sick. That guy talking shit was bad enough, but when that motherfucker kicked my seat, I just couldn't help it. He really fucking pissed me off!"

Brian responds, "Yeah, he was talking a lot of crap, but you still need to control your shit better. The last thing I need is to lose this damn job."

Brian and Mike pull in to the restaurant's parking lot, then go in to grab a burger. After lunch, they go back to the hospital, retrieve Jerome, then head to the station. After they arrive, they handcuff him to a bench, then wait for intake to finish processing him.

As they wait, they decide to go talk to someone else about an unrelated matter. Meanwhile, as Jerome explains what the officers did to him to another inmate, Captain Jon Williams, in his office nearby, overhears him talking. When Mike and Brian come back up front, Captain Williams sees them, comes out of his office, and angrily orders them to come into his office immediately. As Mike and Brian walk into his office, the captain tells them to close the door, then points a finger at them and starts talking in a firm voice.

"I want to talk to you guys. It's my understanding that you were en route, bringing an assault suspect in who was already in custody, in handcuffs and in the back of your car. I'd like you to explain to me how the suspect ended up needing to be transported to the emergency room to have several stitches in his head instead?"

Mike responds, "Yes, Captain, we did have the suspect in custody, but we didn't have his feet restrained. The suspect started losing it in the car, kicking the seat repeatedly. Brian and I warned him to stop, but he wouldn't, so we had to pull over and restrain his feet. When I opened the back door to get him out, the guy started kicking and got me really good in the chest. So, I had to use force to stop him and restrain him and get him to comply. We didn't have any choice." These are, of course, complete lies.

The captain responds, "From my understanding, this guy was almost drunk."

"Yes, the guy was drunk, but also out of control and wouldn't stop kicking," Mike says. "We did what we had to do to restrain him. Yeah, we probably might have used a little more force than we needed to, but this guy had just kicked me in the chest, and I was pissed."

The captain looks at Brian. "Do you have anything to add, Officer Davis?"

Brian responds by lying also. "No, Captain, it happened exactly as Mike described. We gave the suspect every chance, and he just didn't want to listen."

"OK, well, you both need to be advised that the suspect claims he didn't do anything and was just sitting in the back seat when you decided to pull over and beat the shit out of him for no reason. He also claims you started yelling a bunch of racial insults at him. You both better be pretty damn sure about what happened out there. The last thing I need is to have Internal Affairs breathing down my neck because of the actions of you two clowns!"

Even though both officers are completely lying to the captain, Mike takes offense that the captain doesn't believe his lies and starts talking back to him.

"What is this crap? We didn't say shit to this guy other than telling him to sit there and shut the hell up! And then he starts kicking my seat. What the hell was I supposed to do? That scumbag wouldn't listen, so we restrained him, but we didn't say any racial shit to him."

Captain Williams makes it clear he doesn't believe what the officers are saying, mainly because of Mike's history. "Yeah, right, Mike. You think I don't know what you stand for or what you believe? I'm just advising you both that, based on your histories, previous complaints against you, and all the racial crap going on in this city, the last thing this department needs right now is another goddamn story on TV showing white cops beating up on a black suspect – especially one already in custody, with handcuffs on. The city is now probably already looking at a damn lawsuit from this guy. The only thing you both have going in your favor is the fact that the suspect was almost legally drunk."

Mike shoots the captain an angry look, then says, "Look, Captain, I'm tellin' ya –"

Captain Williams interrupts him. "No, I'm tellin' *you*. You two better watch your asses out there, ya' got it?"

Brian tries to calm Mike down. "Yeah, Captain, we got it," he says. "You're dismissed. Get out of my office," orders Captain Williams.

Mike turns to Brian and tells him it's time to go, then storms out of the captain's office. Brian watches him storm out, then walks out himself. As Mike and Brian leave the station to head to their cars, Brian again makes his concerns to Mike clear.

"Mike, you really need to stop this bullshit before you get us both busted."

"Don't worry about it. Jerome isn't gonna be able to prove shit. It's his word against ours. And he had it coming to him after talking shit like he did," Mike says.

"Man, don't try and bullshit me. I'm not fuckin' stupid. That guy wasn't out of control, and he kicked your seat one time after you started talking shit to him about his girlfriend. If you hadn't said anything to him, you wouldn't have gotten him worked up like that. You wanted to beat his ass only because he was talking shit back to you, and because he's black."

Mike rolls his eyes at Brian, then looks at his watch. "Man, I gotta go. Carol's gonna be on my ass if I'm late again. I'll see you later," he says. "Yup. Later," Brian responds.

Mike gets in his car as Brian slowly starts walking to his. As Mike peels out of the parking lot, the look on Brian's face shows he's worried his partner is starting to lose it. Brian then gets in his car and leaves the station to go home.

CHAPTER 5

PHILLIP BATES AT WALMART

Inside the local Walmart, a large line of people with many black people is extending out of the layaway department. A sign at the entrance of the department reads "Layaway Pickup Only. Reminder: All layaways must be picked up by December 15th", which is today. A black female customer approaches the customer service counter. The employee greets her.

"Hello, how may I help you?" the employee asks.

"Yes, hello. I need to pick up this layaway."

She hands the employee her layaway ticket, and the employee enters the ticket number into the computer and sees there's still a balance remaining on the layaway account.

"OK, I see here there's still a remaining balance of $126.54. How would you like to take care of this?"

"I'll pay with cash. Wait…wait a minute…how much did you say that was?" the customer asks.

"$126.54," the employee repeats.

The customer responds, "Uh, no. That can't be right. The amount should be only $26.54. My husband came down last week and made a $100 payment."

The customer service employee tells the customer, "I'm sorry, ma'am, but there's no record of that payment. The last payment I show made was $20, back on December 5th."

The customer appears overwhelmed and confused. "I don't understand that. My husband told me he was going to pay it. What am I supposed to do now? Christmas is only 10 days from now. I don't have $126. He said he was making the payment."

"I'm sorry, ma'am. There's nothing I can do. That payment isn't showing up in the system here. Maybe you can call your husband and ask what happened with the payment?"

"No, I can't call him. My husband died 2 days ago in a car accident. I don't have any money. My kids have already lost their daddy. This layaway was for clothes. I need these clothes for my kids.

They already don't have warm enough clothes as it is. What am I supposed to do now?" she says as she begins crying.

"I'm really very sorry, ma'am. I wish I could do something to help."

Other customers in line look upset at what they're watching, but they aren't in a position to help this poor woman either.

Just then, a voice is heard in the background, near the entrance to the layaway department. "Excuse me, miss."

The customer, the employee, and all the customers in line turn to see Phillip Bates. He's being escorted by a private security officer, the store manager, and his personal assistant, Robert Land.

"I'm going to pay off this woman's layaway," he says.

The customer and employee both have completely shocked looks on their faces as Phillip continues to approach the counter, walking by all the people currently in line.

"I'd also like to pay off the remaining balance of every layaway order currently at this store, including all these people here in line."

The people in line start to cheer and celebrate, excited about their good fortune, then Phillip Bates announces an additional surprise for them.

"Ladies and gentlemen, I realize Christmas is only 10 days away, and I want all of you to have a good, safe, and happy holiday with your families and loved ones. There's nothing more important in your lives than family and friends. Money will come and go. Jobs will come and go. But the people you love will always be what is the most important in your lives."

Phillip turns to face the customer, then takes her hand and looks into her face, speaking to her directly.

"Even if sometimes they can't be with us in person. Here, I want you to have this. It's Christmas. Your kids will have their new clothes, but I want you to buy them something extra nice for Christmas that'll help make their Christmas just a little bit more special."

Phillip hands her a $100 Walmart gift card, and she cries and hugs him, then thanks him as she continues to cry.

"Thank you. Thank you so much, sir. God bless you. You've just saved my life."

"You're very welcome, ma'am. Now you can pick up your clothes and then go shopping."

Phillip turns to the line and crowd of additional customers and employees that have gathered at the entrance of the layaway department to see what was going on, then announces his gift to the crowd.

"Folks, I want you all to have a really great Christmas. I'm giving each one of you here a $100 gift card to help you celebrate the holiday this year. Merry Christmas to all of you."

The crowd erupts in cheers, all very happy and surprised at his generosity. Phillip lets them cheer for a minute, then raises his hands and motions for the crowd to please quiet down. Everyone quickly quiets down to listen to what else he has to say. Phillip then turns to face the store manager, Mr. White.

"Mr. White, I'd appreciate it if you'd have your staff make the appropriate phone calls to the remaining layaway customers who aren't here in line to tell them their layaway items have been paid in full and are ready for pickup, along with a $100 gift card for each of them. Please get the final total for all expenses to my associate here, Robert Land. He'll get it paid."

He hands Mr. White a business card, and the manager says he'll see to it right away as an excited look dawns on his face. Phillip tells him that for his efforts, he's going to give a $500 cash bonus both to him and every employee of the store for Christmas. The customer service employee is completely shocked and comes out from behind the counter to give Phillip a hug and thank him. Mr. White is also shocked at what Phillip is doing for his people, and he shakes Phillip's hand and thanks him.

"Thank you, Mr. Bates. I can't thank you enough for my family, employees, and customers. You've given me a new reason to believe in Santa Claus."

Phillip tells him he's very kind, then walks up to the first person in the front of the layaway line and puts his hand out to his assistant, Robert. Robert pulls out a large stack of gift cards and hands it to Phillip, who goes down the line, giving each person a $100 gift card. Some customers shake his hand, while others give him a hug and thank him. After giving cards to all the people in line, he heads over and starts giving cards to each of the customers standing around, watching the scene. After he gives the last person a card, Phillip turns to face the crowd and tells them all to have a Merry Christmas and great holiday season. The crowd cheers and gives him a round of applause. In response, he waves to them, then leaves the store. Once outside, Phillip and Robert get in their car, with Robert driving.

Robert says, "That was really great, sir. Those people were very happy. So, where would you like to go now?"

"I don't know about you, but I'm starving. Are you hungry?" Phillip asks.

"Yeah, I'm pretty hungry, too. You want to go grab some lunch somewhere?"

"Yeah, how about that little café on Main Street?" Phillip responds.

He and Robert then head toward the Main Street Café.

CHAPTER 6

MURPHY CONFRONTS TEENAGERS

Officer Mike Murphy is arriving at his home after leaving the police department, having been warned by his captain, Jon Williams, about his actions towards Jerome Goshen.

Mike isn't in a good mood. As he comes driving down the street and pulls into the driveway of his small house, he sees two black teenagers doing yard work, raking leaves, in the front yard. He pulls into his driveway, gets out of the car, and walks towards his front door. Both teenagers stop working and just give him a blank stare, as if they seem to know him. He just stares at them without saying a word as he continues into the house.

Mike's wife, Carol, is sitting on the couch on her laptop with the TV on, showing the current weather. She smiles when she sees him and asks him how work was today; she's in a good mood. Mike stops just inside the doorway in front of her and looks down at her with an angry look on his face.

"Why are there are two fuckin' niggers in our front yard?" he snaps.

The look on Carol's face changes from smiling and happy to angry as she gets up from the couch. "They're cleaning the damn yard! You were never gonna get it done. I've been asking you to do it for the last two weeks. What's the problem?" she asks.

"I don't want any fuckin' niggers in my yard, and I certainly don't want my money going to pay for their shit either. *That's* the fucking problem!" Mike responds.

"Fine. You can be the one to tell them to leave, then. And then you can do the fuckin' yard yourself!" Carol yells.

Mike gives her an angry look, then goes storming out the front door to talk to the teenagers. As he walks up to them, they stop working when they see him coming.

Still wearing his full police uniform and belt with his firearm, he looks at them both and says, "Hey, you niggers beat it. We don't need your help here anymore. I got this."

Stunned, both teens look pissed that he's used such language with them. The larger teenager, Trey, asks about the money Carol had promised them.

The smaller teenager then says, "Yeah, she promised us 20 bucks each when we got done cleaning this yard."

Mike says, "Yeah, well, you didn't finish the fuckin' yard, did you?" He hands Trey $10 out of his wallet. "Here. Here's ten bucks. Take it and get the fuck out of here."

Trey grabs the $10 bill, then looks at Mike and says, "Punk-ass thief."

This absolutely infuriates Mike. His eyes open wide, and he looks like he's about to beat the crap out of the kid. He gets right up in his face and starts yelling.

"What the fuck did you just call me? You're gonna want to watch what the fuck you say to me, you fucking little monkey, or you're gonna find your ass in jail. You wanna go to jail? Huh? You wanna go to jail right now?!" Mike yells.

Not wanting any trouble with the officer, the smaller teenager tells Trey, "C'mon, Trey, let's bounce."

Mike, still up in the Trey's face, says, "YEAH, TREY! BOUNCE the fuck outta here, off my property, before I bounce your little black ass off myself."

Trey gives Mike a dirty look, then looks down at his gun, realizing it's probably better to leave than start fighting with a police officer in full uniform, wearing his gun. He backs up, then turns around and both teens walk away. As Mike goes back into the house, he sees Carol standing by the front door, watching everything.

"That was pretty damn mean out there. Those kids hadn't done a damn thing to you and were just looking to earn some cash. And that yard looks like shit. It needed to be done anyway," she says.

Mike starts screaming at her. "Hey, BULLSHIT! You don't hire that kind of shit EVER again, OK?! I don't get up, go to work, and deal with those fucking monkeys all day just to come home and have to deal with them at MY OWN FUCKING HOUSE!"

Carol gives him a mean look, then storms off into the bedroom. Mike goes into the kitchen to get a beer out of the fridge. Carol comes back out of the bedroom with her purse on her shoulder.

"Where the hell are you going?" he demands.

"I'm going out with friends. I don't want to be here with you right now. You're being a real asshole."

Mike says, "Yeah, whatever. Go ahead. Get the hell out."

He waves his hand like he's swatting her away like a fly, then looks at her and says sarcastically, "BOUNCE!"

Carol storms out the front door, slamming the door shut on her way out.

Mike sits down on the couch and grabs the TV remote to put on the local news while drinking his beer. Before long, a news story comes on, showing what Phillip Bates had just done at Walmart with the gift cards.

Reporter Melissa Childs is outside the Walmart, in the parking lot.

"Earlier today, Phillip Bates came into this store and surprised every customer in the store with a $100 gift card to purchase Christmas gifts. He also paid off every layaway balance in this store. The store manager has just confirmed to me that all layaway balances are now paid in full. If you have an item on layaway here, you must come in to the store by closing time tonight to pick up the item."

Standing with Melissa is Shenequa Brown, one of the customers who received a gift card and had her layaway balance paid off by Phillip. Shenequa is a black woman.

"I'm standing here with Miss Shenequa Brown, who was in the store in the layaway department when Phillip Bates came in. Now Shenequa, can you tell us what it was like when Mr. Bates first came in? What did he say?"

Right when Melissa says Shenequa's name and the woman is shown on TV, Mike rolls his eyes, shakes his head, and says, "It figures. Fucking niggers. I swear to God."

Shenequa explains what happened when Phillip came in. "Well, I was standing in line to pick up my layaway gift for my son for Christmas, and there was this lady trying to pick up her item at the front of the line, up by the counter, but she didn't have enough money to pay for it. She thought her husband had made a payment before or something. The woman started crying, and there was nothing the store could do. I mean, they couldn't just give it to her. Then Mr. Bates showed up out of the blue at the back of the line and said he was gonna pay for her layaway. Then he turned around and looked at us all and said he was gonna pay for everyone else's layaways also. Then he gave her a $100 gift card and then started passing out $100 gift cards to everyone in line, including me. It just made my day. Mr. Bates is like an angel or something, because people just don't do that around here. But he does. I just wish there were more people like that around here."

Mike rolls his eyes again and says to himself, "Yeah, more people to give you a fuckin' handout, huh? Why don't ya' get a fuckin' job instead for a change?!"

Melissa says, "And there you have it, folks. Another early gift from one of the most generous men in the community. From Walmart, I'm Melissa Childs, reporting for WESH News mid-day."

The TV cuts back to the studio, where the reporters have been watching her report.

"Wow. Phillip Bates's generosity never ceases to amaze me. Now, on to our next story, also involving Phillip Bates. The town's annual Christmas celebration and tree lighting ceremony will be taking place this evening in the town square courtyard. The Phillip Bates Foundation has donated all the money to pay for the ceremony, the food, and the entire event. The event will be starting this evening at 6 PM."

The other anchor says, "That will be a great event, and we hope to see you there."

The first anchor then says, "You know, much of the budget for the city and police and fire departments comes from the Phillip Bates Foundation. Have a great evening, folks. We'll be back on the air tonight at 6 PM."

Mike just stares at the TV, having just heard how Phillip Bates funds the department where he works. The news ends, and as the music for the end of the broadcast starts playing, Mike puts down his beer and gets the laptop Carol had been using on the couch when he came home. He puts it on his lap, then types in the name of a website, www.mightyplace.com.

CHAPTER 7

MAIN STREET CAFÉ ACCIDENT

Phillip and Robert drive down Main Street towards the Main Street Café to get lunch. The café is on the left side of the road, and parking is behind the café. As they get close to the café, they come upon a traffic accident right in front of the building. Apparently, a car had turned left in front of another car, and the oncoming car had crashed right into the passenger side of the car turning left. A police officer is directing traffic, which is backed up several cars down the road.

Irritated with the traffic, Phillip says, "Oh God, not again."

Robert responds, "This is the fourth accident at this intersection in the last month."

Phillip says, "Yes, it is. Bob, remind me to bring this up at the city council meeting tomorrow. I want a traffic light here at this intersection. This is ridiculous."

After about five minutes, they finally make it to the front of the line of traffic, and the police officer directs them to go ahead and make their turn onto the street heading behind the restaurant towards the parking lot. As they're turning onto the street, they notice an older lady with her daughter standing on the corner, looking at the car that had crashed into the side of the left-turning car. The woman is crying. The car was an older model, and not in the best shape. It's clear from the make, model, and appearance of the car that the woman doesn't have a lot of money. The left-turning car had already been towed away from the scene.

Robert and Phillip park in the parking lot, then Robert looks at Phillip and says, "You're gonna help her, aren't you?"

Phillip nods yes, then tells Robert to give him a "10 Pack". Robert reaches into the back seat under a blanket, pulls out a case, and opens it. The case is filled with stacks of cash, and he grabs a stack of $100 bills with a label around it saying "$10,000", then hands it to Phillip. He then closes the case and puts it back under the blanket in the back seat.

Both men get out of the car and head towards the front of the restaurant, where the entrance is located. As they approach the woman, who's still crying and being comforted by a police officer, Phillip overhears her conversation.

"I needed that car to get to work. I don't have insurance for it, and I don't have any money to get it fixed either. How am I supposed to get to work now? How am I supposed to even go to the store now?"

Phillip walks up behind the woman and stands quietly. Her daughter sees Phillip and taps her mom to get her attention, saying "Mom, look."

The woman turns around to see Phillip standing behind her. He takes off the hat he's wearing to greet her. "Pardon me, Miss, but I couldn't help overhearing what you were saying to this officer. Was this your car?"

"Yes, sir, it was," she responds.

"And you have no insurance to repair the damage?"

"No, sir, not for collision," she responds.

"What's your name, Miss?"

"My name is Dorothy Watts."

"Well, Dorothy, I want to help you. Give me your hand."

She looks at the police officer, who already seems to have an idea of what's happening, as he appears to know Phillip and his reputation. The officer nods to Dorothy that it's okay to give him her hand, and she nervously puts out her hand, as if to shake Phillip's; however, instead of shaking her hand, he grabs it by the back and rotates it so her palm is facing upright, then pulls the $10,000 out of his coat pocket and places it in her hand, holding on to it.

While holding both her hands, he looks directly into her face and says, "Get your car repaired, Dorothy, or buy a new car, okay? Everything will be fine. Don't let this little mishap ruin a wonderful day."

Dorothy starts crying and gives Phillip a big hug. "Thank you. Thank you so much, sir."

"You're welcome, ma'am. You can thank me by having a wonderful Christmas with your daughter and family."

Robert and the police officer have big smiles on their faces. The police officer extends his hand to shake Phillip's, then thanks him for helping Dorothy. Phillip tells the officer he's doing great work.

Behind Phillip and Robert are several customers of the diner, watching out the window. They see what Phillip's just done for Dorothy.

"Dorothy, deposit that money into the bank immediately, okay? You don't want to be carrying that kind of cash around in public. You have a Merry Christmas," Phillip says.

She responds by wishing him a Merry Christmas, too, then says, "God bless you."

Phillip and Robert head into the diner. As they enter, the customers give Phillip a round of applause for what he's just done.

He says to everyone, "Thank you, folks. Now, we're all here for some lunch, right?" He looks at the hostess. "Put everyone's bill here on my tab." He then looks around at the customers. "Your lunches are all on me today. And I hope you'll all join me this evening at the tree lighting ceremony at 6 PM, in the town square down the street. Now please, everyone, enjoy your lunches."

Phillip and Robert are taken to a booth themselves, and several customers thank Phillip for the free lunch as they walk to their booth, where they sit down and are given menus.

Robert asks Phillip, "Sir, how are you able to do it?"

"Do what? What are you talking about?" Phillip asks.

"How are you able to bring out the best in people? Everywhere you go, people are happy, and you're the reason why. How are you able to do that?"

Phillip looks directly at Robert in a way that makes it appear that it is a dumb question and says, "It's called money, Robert!"

Robert's cell phone rings. "Hello? (pause) Yes, it is. No, Phillip isn't available at the moment, but I'll give him the message. Yeah. Thank you. Goodbye." He ends the call. "That was the news people calling again. They really want an interview with you, especially after the Walmart thing this morning."

Phillip says, "I definitely need to give them an 'A' for persistence."

"Yeah. But maybe you should consider talking to them. You know, some folks might think you're just doing what you're doing for attention. Maybe this would provide a good chance to explain to the people what you're doing," Robert says.

Phillip responds, "And what do you think it is I'm doing? You think I'm just doing this for attention?"

"No, of course not. Look Phil, I've known you for over 30 years now. I know you love to help people. But it doesn't matter what you do or how many people you help. There will always be someone out there who'll think something else is going on. It's just human nature. Most people just can't understand giving away money like that to complete strangers without expecting something in return. This is your chance to explain to some of those people that you just like to help people and never expect anything in return."

"Do you think I should do the interview?" Phillip asks.

Robert says, "Yes, I do think so. I think it'll help people understand and appreciate you more."

Phillip responds, "Fine. Go ahead and get the interview set up."

Robert says he'll try to get it set up for some time in the next couple of days.

Phillip says, "That's fine. Now, let's get some food. Remember, I told Mary we'd be home to pick her up around 5 for the tree lighting ceremony."

CHAPTER 8

TREE LIGHTING CEREMONY

Melissa Childs is reporting live from the tree lighting ceremony.

"OK, it looks like Mayor Steve Wilson is about to wrap up his speech, then he'll be introducing Phillip Bates to the podium. Mr. Bates apparently has a special announcement to make. And in case you aren't familiar with Phillip Bates, his company is the largest employer in the state. The Phillip Bates Foundation has graciously provided funding for numerous public projects and events, including this ceremony. Earlier today, we reported from Walmart, where Phillip Bates had come into the store and paid off all remaining layaway balances for customers and gave every single customer in the store a $100 gift card for Christmas. Let's listen in now as the mayor announces him to the stage."

The mayor announces, "And so, without further ado, I'd like to welcome our most generous contributor, who's made this evening here possible, Mr. Phillip Bates."

The crowd erupts in cheers and applause, as they're all very well aware of what Phillip has done for the city. Phillip and his wife, Mary had been standing behind the Mayor. He walks away from his wife and steps up to the podium to start speaking. Several city officials are also up on stage, standing behind Phillip. The area around the stage has hundreds of people who have come to attend the ceremony and see the Christmas tree being lit.

Phillip begins his speech by thanking several people. He offers thanks to the mayor and city council members for their help in making the event possible. He also thanks all the volunteers who have generously provided their time and energy to help prepare for the ceremony. Phillip then waves to his wife, standing behind him next to the mayor, to come up and join him. As Mary walks up next to Phillip, he takes her hand and looks at her.

"And finally, I want to thank the love of my life, my beautiful wife, Mary. Her continued inspiration, love, and support of me and all of you is what keeps pushing me to continue to help all of you."

He tells Mary he loves her, gives her a kiss, then continues.

"And while all the people on this stage and volunteers here have helped prepare for this ceremony, this entire event would not be taking place if it weren't for all of you people. Neither I, any of the people on this stage, nor the volunteers are the reason we're here at this ceremony. The reason we're here is because of all of you people, who support this event by coming out every year to see the Christmas tree lighting."

The crowd again applauds him.

"Now, I have one last item to announce before we light this tree. Christmas is just 10 days away now, and I have an early Christmas gift to present to this city. Working with the mayor and city council members, I'm happy to report that in just two weeks we'll be breaking ground on Bates Community College. More details will be coming soon, but I wanted to announce classes at the school will always be free for everyone." As the crowd starts going crazy, cheering wildly, Phillip shouts over the crowd, "Merry Christmas to all of you, and have a great, safe, and happy holiday. Let's start the countdown now."

The crowd starts to count down from 10 to 0. When they get to 0, the tree lights up, then everyone cheers again. Phillip kisses his wife again and puts his arm around her, then hears a voice behind him calling his name. He turns to face the mayor and council members who want to shake his hand and congratulate him on the successful tree lighting ceremony, as well as for the college announcement.

Melissa Childs finishes her report, giving details about Phillip's announcement. "And there you have it, folks. Phillip Bates has just announced the construction, starting in two weeks, of a new community college that will offer free classes. Now we've been given some additional information I'm now allowed to report. The college will offer all classes free to residents of this state. Students will only be responsible for purchasing their books; however, students can earn credits that can be used to purchase books by performing several different types of community service. They'll be able to sign up for the community service and be given plenty of time to complete it prior to any classes starting. The college will offer all general education classes, as well as specific programs for associate degrees. There will also be several programs to earn training for various trades, such as truck driving, EMT, plumbing, construction, electrician, dental assistant, and many more. A full list will be available soon. Now, this college will be located just down the road from here, about a mile away, on a 25-acre parcel of land next to the McDonalds. Over the next several weeks and months ahead, there will be more information coming about the new college. And that's the big news here tonight. Reporting from town square, I'm Melissa Childs, for WESH News, Evening."

The camera turns off, and an assistant to Melissa comes up to her to tell her she did a great job.

CHAPTER 9

CITY COUNCIL MEETING

Downtown, at one of the city offices, a private city council meeting is in progress. Several city council members are present, as well as the mayor, chief of police, and local district attorney and superior court judge. Everyone is seated around a large rectangular-shaped table. Phillip Bates is seated at one end of the table, with Robert Land in a chair behind him.

The council foreman is about to wrap the meeting and asks if there are any more items that need to be discussed.

Phillip says, "Yes," then directs his attention at Police Chief Dan Brady. "I have a question for Dan. I want to know what happened yesterday regarding an incident in which a Mr. Jerome Goshen was placed under arrest by police officers."

Dan responds, "Yes, sir. We'd received a call from a woman claiming her boyfriend, Jerome, was drinking and threatening her. Two police officers, Mike Murphy and Brian Davis, responded, arriving at the residence about 10 minutes later to find Mr. Goshen assaulting his girlfriend. They made entry into the premises, placed Jerome under arrest, took him out, and placed him in the back seat of their car. Apparently, en route to the station, the suspect became belligerent and violent in the back seat and started kicking the back of the car seat in front of him. So, the officers pulled over to the side of the road and pulled the suspect out of the car to restrain his feet. In the process of removing Mr. Goshen from the car, he kicked Officer Murphy in the chest pretty hard. Murphy became very angry and used his nightstick on the suspect until the suspect stopped resisting. Unfortunately, in the process Mr. Goshen sustained an injury to his face that required some stitches at the hospital. Both officers were questioned about the incident by Captain Jon Williams, and both gave the exact same description of the events."

Phillip responds, "I was told the suspect reported to the hospital that he was beaten by these two officers for no reason. That they decided just to pull over and beat him, unprovoked, and even made several racially sensitive statements to the suspect in the process. Is this correct?"

"I'm aware of the suspect's comments. The suspect was intoxicated, very near the legal limit. And the fact that both officers gave the same report makes it really a case of his word against the word of two officers with several years of experience on the force," Dan responds.

Phillip says, "I'd like you to personally keep an eye on these two officers. Keep them in line. There are already enough race-related issues going on in this city, as well as other cities. I don't want another race-related issue to give this city a black eye."

Phillip clearly has a lot of clout within this group of people, as he talks to Dan in a way that makes it sound like an order. Dan tells Phillip he'll keep an eye on the two officers. The council foreman then asks if anyone else has anything further. Robert taps Phillip on the shoulder to get his attention, then as Phillip leans back, he whispers into his ear to remind him about the traffic light.

Phillip thanks Robert for reminding him about it, then says, "Yes, one more item I'd like to discuss. Robert and I went to the Main Street Café for lunch yesterday. At the intersection by the entrance, a traffic accident was being cleaned up. This is the fourth traffic accident I'm aware of in less than a month at this intersection. I want a traffic light with a left turn arrow installed at this intersection. I'll add the cost to my monthly foundation budget for the city to cover it."

The council foreman looks around at everyone and asks if anyone has any objection to this. One of the other council members comments that this intersection has needed a traffic light for a long time. The council foreman tells Phillip since there are no objections, they'll make the arrangements with the local Department of Transportation to get the light installed. The council foreman then says the mayor would like to make a final announcement before they adjourn.

The mayor says, "Thank you. On behalf of this council, I just want to take this opportunity to offer my sincerest thanks to Phillip Bates for the festival last night, and to congratulate him on the community college announcement. It appears the crowd was quite pleased with the announcement. This city is forever in your debt, sir."

The council members applaud Phillip.

"Thank you all very much. I consider you all very good friends. I've lived in this city for many years, and this city is my home. I'll always do everything I can to protect my home and make improvements everyone can enjoy. The community college will be a wonderful addition to the city, but I have something even greater planned to help the people of the city. I'll be ready to discuss it very soon. Now if you'll excuse me, I have to meet my wife, Mary, for lunch. I wish you all a wonderful holiday."

As Phillip and Robert leave the meeting, the council foreman announces the meeting is adjourned and thanks everyone for coming, as well as wishes them a wonderful holiday. He ends by telling them he'll see them all next month.

CHAPTER 10

CHURCH BURGLARY

Christ's Community Church on Jasper Drive is a small but well-established church. It held a fundraiser earlier in the day and had also taken in several Christmas gifts for children who otherwise wouldn't be getting anything for Christmas.

It's after midnight, and the church pastor, Jason Alexander, is on his way back to the church from a meeting he'd attended earlier in the evening. Two black teenagers are casing the church around the outside, and they come to a window on a side of the church that's not very well-lit. One of the teenagers has on a red baseball cap and blue jeans. Both teens look into the window, then look around to make sure nobody is watching them or coming.

One of them says to the other, "Okay, do it now."

The second teenager closest to the window breaks the window, then clears off the pieces of glass and climbs into the window. The first teenager follows him into the window.

Once inside the church, the young men look around, then eventually come to an office with a metal cash box on the desk that says "Donations". The second teenager, wearing the red baseball cap, opens the box and reveals it's stuffed with cash from the donations earlier in the day.

He calls the first teenager over and says, "Hey man, look at this."

"Holy shit, dude," replies the other. "There must be over a thousand bucks in the box."

"Damn. Take it, and let's get the fuck outta here."

The teenager with the red cap grabs all the cash and puts it in his pocket. There's so much of it, it's difficult for him to stuff it all in. Both teens then quickly make their way out of the room and back towards the broken window. The first teen climbs out of the window, and the second one follows out right behind him.

As the teens come out on the other side, Pastor Jason Alexander is pulling into the parking lot. He gets out of the car and hears the noise from the teens exiting the building and stepping on the broken glass on the ground. He runs around the side of the church to investigate, and as he comes around the corner, he sees the two teens, particularly the face of the teen wearing the red baseball cap.

As both teens run in the opposite direction, away from the pastor, he chases them while yelling at them to stop. When he gets to the broken window, he stops to look inside. The teens are now gone, having run off into the dark, and Jason is very upset as he looks inside the window. He takes out his cell phone and dials 911 to report the break-in.

"9-1-1, what is your emergency?"

"Yes. Hello. My name is Jason Alexander. I'm the pastor of the Christ's Community Church on Jasper Drive. I just arrived at the church and found two teenagers coming out of a window on the side of the building. They'd just broken into the place."

"OK, hold on. Let me get officers on the way to you right now. Can you describe the suspects?"

"Yes. It was two men, both black males. They looked kinda young, maybe in their late teens or early twenties. One of them was wearing a red baseball cap and blue jeans."

"OK, the officers are on the way there now. They're very close. Are you in the front of the church?"

"No, ma'am, I'm on the side of the building by the broken window they were coming out of."

"OK, go to the front of the church. The officers should be pulling up now."

Jason walks around the side of the building and sees the police car pulling into the parking lot. "Yes, I see them now. They're here. Thank you."

"OK, you take care of yourself now, sir."

"Yes, thank you."

Just as Jason hangs up the phone, a police car arrives and Officers Davis and Murphy get out. As Jason walks up to the officers, Mike questions him.

"Are you the person who called to report the break-in?"

Jason confirms he's the person who made the call and takes the officers around the side of the church to show them the broken window he'd seen the teens coming out of.

"I chased them, but they got away," he says.

"OK. Can you give us any description of them?" Mike asks.

"Yes, I got a good look at one of them. They were both young black males, maybe in their teens or early 20s. One had blue jeans and was wearing a red baseball cap."

"OK. Have you been inside the church?" Mike asks.

"No, I haven't. I wasn't sure if there might be more of them in there or not and wanted to wait for you."

"OK. Is the front door unlocked?"

"Yes, this house of God is always open to everyone."

"So, these guys broke a window to enter an open church that had the front door unlocked?" Mike says. Then, looking at Brian, he says, "Obviously not the brightest bulbs in the lamp, huh?" He tells Jason, "OK, wait out front by our car while we go in and make sure there aren't any other suspects inside the building."

Jason waits by the patrol car as Mike and Brian head inside the front door of the church, with their guns drawn. They're inside for a few minutes, then Jason sees a light come on in the room where the broken window is located on the side of the building. He keeps looking around for the two teens to see if they come back, but they're long gone.

After another minute, the officers come out of the church. They approach Jason to tell him the building is clear, then ask him if he'd like to come inside to see if anything is missing. He says yes, then the officers escort him into the church. Jason immediately heads to his office, where the box with the money was located. As he enters the room, he's shocked and furious at the sight of the money box open on his desk and all the money gone.

* * *

The next morning, Phillip Bates is watching the local news at home when a story comes on about the church robbery. The studio anchor explains how the church was robbed and the thieves got away with something very valuable. The broadcast then switches to Melissa Childs, who's standing by live at the scene.

"I'm standing here at the Christ's Community Church, with Pastor Jason Alexander, where the two thieves broke into the church earlier this evening. The thieves got away with almost $4,000. This money had been donated for the Christmas presents that were going to be purchased tomorrow for families in the community that can't afford to purchase gifts for their children. Pastor Alexander, can you tell us what happened here tonight?"

Jason explains exactly what happened and gives a complete description of what the suspects looked like. "I don't know what I'm going to do now. We've worked so hard to collect this money. Christmas is less than a week away, and we'd planned on buying the Christmas gifts tomorrow. Now we won't be able to do that anymore."

Melissa responds, "I am really very sorry to hear this has happened. I feel sorry for the kids who are now going to miss out on what could have been a Christmas they'd never forget. Now, unfortunately, they may still never forget this Christmas, but for the wrong reason. Anyone with any information related to this case is urged to call the police immediately."

Phillip watches the end of the report before the channel goes to a commercial. He then picks up the phone and calls the TV station.

"Yes, hello. This is Phillip Bates. I'd like to be connected with the newsroom regarding your current story about the church, please."

Phillip is connected with a producer in the newsroom, explains how he wants to help the church, and ends the call. The commercial break ends, and the news broadcast resumes with the studio anchor.

"Prior to the commercial break, we were reporting on the burglary at the Christ's Community Church. During the break, we received some new information regarding this case. We're now going back live to Melissa Childs at the church."

"I'm standing here with Pastor Jason Alexander, who earlier explained to us how thieves broke into the church and stole over $4,000 that had been donated for Christmas. This money had been planned for the purchase of Christmas gifts for needy families tomorrow, correct, Pastor Alexander?" Melissa reports.

Jason responds, "That's right, Melissa. We really lost a lot of money today."

"Well, Pastor Alexander, during the commercial break we received a phone call at the station from one of our viewers. Phillip Bates just happened to be watching the broadcast and called in to the station to say he's immediately donating $10,000 to your church to purchase the gifts for the children."

Jason starts crying, in complete shock about the amount of the donation.

Mike Murphy is off camera, still at the scene, and is also surprised to hear the amount of the donation.

Jason says, "Oh my goodness. Wow, that's really great. Mr. Phillip Bates, thank you so much from the bottom of my heart. You have no idea what a difference this is going to make for these kids. Thank you, and God bless you, sir."

Melissa says, "And Mr. Bates, I think I can speak for all of us at WESH when I say thank you for your help. That is really an incredible gift to the church. A lot of children will be happy this Christmas. Reporting live for WESH News, this is Melissa Childs."

CHAPTER 11

HOUSE FIRE

On Timber Ridge Drive, a quiet residential street in town, many houses are decorated with Christmas lights. It's 2 AM, and a small house on the street has the curtains in its front window open so people driving by can see the Christmas tree lit up at night.

Suddenly, a small flash sparks in the window, right where the tree is located. Within seconds, an orange glow starts to grow brighter at the bottom of the tree. The lights on the Christmas tree have just shorted out and set it on fire.

In the master bedroom, Sarah Carter is sleeping. She's startled awake by the sounds of the fire alarm going off and her dog barking in her room. As her cat jumps on her chest, scared from the sounds of the dog and fire alarm, she smells smoke and sees the orange glow of light coming into the room from the hallway.

She jumps out of bed and heads into the hallway. The smoke in the hall is very thick, but she's able to see through it into the living room, where she can see the entire Christmas tree now engulfed in flames.

Sarah wastes no time. She bursts into the bedroom of her son, Mikey, gets him out of bed, and tells him to grab his shoes and a coat out of the closet immediately. He gets his coat and shoes, then they both head back into the hallway.

The smoke is now way too thick, and the heat in the living room is very intense and too dangerous to risk trying to go into the front room to get out of the house. So, Sarah leads Mikey into the master bedroom. After looking around and seeing both her dog and cat in the room, she shuts the bedroom door. She then takes Mikey into the master bathroom and opens a window. After pushing out the screen, she helps lift him out of the window, then goes into the bedroom, gets her cell phone, cat, and dog, and pushes both the animals out the window. She then escapes out the window herself.

Once outside, Sarah and Mikey go around the back of the house towards the front and out into the street, where she calls 911.

The 911 operator answers. "Nine-one-one, what is your emergency?"

Sarah says, "Yes, my house is on fire. Our Christmas tree caught fire. Please send the fire department quickly."

The operator says, "OK, ma'am."

Sarah says, "Oh God, please help me."

The operator tells Sarah, "Ma'am, I need you to stop and listen to me. What is your address?"

"It's 2015 Timber Ridge Drive. Please hurry."

"OK, ma'am, the fire department is on the way. Is everyone out of the house?"

"Yes, everyone is out of the house. Are they almost here?"

"Yes, ma'am, they're getting close," the operator says. "What is your name?"

"What was that?" Sarah asks.

"Your name, ma'am. What is your name?"

"Oh. It's Sarah Carter," she says, panicking as she watches her house go up in flames.

The operator says, "OK, Sarah, is anyone hurt?"

"No. I don't think so. But my house is burning."

"OK. And you said the fire started by the Christmas tree?"

"Yes, I was sleeping and my cat jumped on me and my dog started barking and the smoke detector started going off and I woke up and could smell smoke. And I went into the hallway and saw the tree on fire in the living room."

"OK, Sarah, the fire department will be there in about one minute."

Just then, the truck from the fire department pulls up to the scene, then the firemen scramble out and start grabbing hoses to prepare to fight the fire.

* * *

The following morning, Phillip and Mary are watching the news as their butler, George Boyer, serves them breakfast. A story comes on about the fire at Sara's house. Melissa Childs is at the house, reporting on the fire. She's with Sarah.

"The house here on Timber Ridge Drive appears to be a complete loss after the family Christmas tree caught fire in the living room. The family was sleeping at the time, and though they were able to make it safely out of the home, the house and all contents, including the Christmas presents, are a total loss." She turns to Sarah. "Sarah, can you explain what happened and how you were awakened to find your house on fire?"

"Well, I was sleeping, then all of a sudden the dog started barking and the cat jumped on my chest and the smoke detector started going off. So, I jumped out of bed and ran into the hallway and could see the Christmas tree and the whole room on fire. I went into my son's room and got him out of bed and grabbed his shoes and jacket and took him into the bedroom to help him out the window. Once we got out, I called for help."

"OK, and I understand you had pets? Do you know what happened with them?" Melissa asks.

"Yeah, we have a dog named 'Buster' and a cat. I got them both out of the house, too."

"This fire occurred around 2 o'clock this morning. I know you've been here the entire time, ever since the fire department left a couple of hours ago. Have you been able to recover anything from the house?"

"I was able to get a picture of my baby sister, who died a few years ago. But that's about it. Everything else is completely gone," Sarah says, crying.

"I'm so sorry for your loss," Melissa asks. "At least your insurance should be able to cover your losses, right?"

"No, I don't have any insurance. It was canceled last month. I couldn't afford the payment. They wanted the full payment up front for the whole year. But I have my son and my dog and cat, and that's what matters most to me right now. I don't have a home, but we have each other. I put my trust in God to help me with the rest."

"Well, I am very sorry for your loss, Sarah. Hopefully, some of our viewers might be able to help out. We've set up a GoFundMe page to help Sarah, and the link to donate to help her can be found on our website, WESHTV.com."

As Melissa concludes her report on the fire, Phillip turns to Mary. "Mary, I'd like to pay for a new house and Christmas presents for her. What do you think?"

Mary looks at him, with a big smile on her face. "Do you know just how much I love you? I think you're the most generous, wonderful person I've ever known, and I think rebuilding her house for her is a great idea. It'll be the best Christmas present she and her son have ever received in their lives."

Phillip responds, "I love you, too. And I think you're the most beautiful, caring woman I've ever known. I couldn't be any happier than I am when I'm with you. Would you like to get dressed and go with me to tell Sarah we'll rebuild her house?"

Mary says she'd love to go and she'll get dressed and be ready in about twenty minutes. As she gets up to leave the room, Phillip calls out to George, who comes into the room and asks him what he needs. Phillip asks him to have Robert bring the car around in front of the house in about fifteen minutes. George then goes off to find Robert as Phillip gets up to go get dressed and get ready to leave himself.

* * *

Later, at Sarah's house, she and her son are still looking through the rubble, with the help of her neighbors. A pile of items has been pulled from the rubble, and as everyone searches through it, a limousine pulls up to the house. Sarah sees the car pull up, and as it comes to a stop, Phillip and Mary get out. A look of surprise comes over Sarah's face as she recognizes Phillip. She calls Mikey over to her, then they walk down the driveway toward Phillip and Mary, who approach them in kind. As Phillip takes off his hat to greet Sarah, the neighbors walk up behind her to see what's going on.

"Good afternoon, Sarah. My name is Phillip Bates. This is my wife, Mary. We saw your story on the news this morning," he says.

Sarah smiles and shakes their hands. "Hello. I'm very happy to meet you. I feel like I know you already. I've seen so many stories about you on the news. This is my son, Mikey."

Phillip bends down to say hello to Mikey, who's scared and shy and moves behind Sarah. Phillip smiles, then stands back up to speak to Sarah, with Mary standing right next to him.

"Sarah, my wife and I would like to help you." Sarah's eyes open wide. "We're going to build a brand new house for you and Mikey."

Sarah quickly puts both hands over her mouth and starts crying. "Oh my God!" she exclaims. "Oh my God, are you serious? You're really, seriously going to rebuild my house? You're not joking?" she asks.

Phillip responds, "We are absolutely serious. This is no joke. We also have something else for you."

Mary hands Sarah an envelope containing $5,000 in cash.

"This is for your immediate needs. It's for food, new clothes, and Christmas gifts for you and Mikey," Phillip says.

Sarah is completely shocked at what's happening to her.

"Now, it may take a few months to rebuild your house. So, while you're waiting for it to be completed, we'll provide a nice apartment for you and Mikey to live in. You can pick out the apartment, and we'll cover the full rent and all utilities and expenses until your new house is ready for you to move in. OK?"

Still crying, Sarah thanks them both, then hugs each of them in turn. The neighbors behind them are smiling, and Phillip and Mary are also both smile while hugging Sarah. Phillip then hands Sarah a business card.

"This card is for my associate here, Mr. Robert Land. He'll help you with everything you may need. We already have a hotel room at the Marriott down the street, booked and paid for, ready for you to check in. The room is pre-paid for a week while you and Mikey look for an apartment. Give Robert a call tomorrow. He'll be expecting your call."

Phillip puts his hat back on as Sarah, still crying, says she'll give Robert a call in the morning. She thanks them again, then tells them, "God bless you both."

Phillip tells her and Mikey he hopes they have a Merry Christmas and Happy New Year, then tips his hat to the neighbors and turns to head back towards his car. Suddenly, he turns back around.

"Oh, Sarah, I forgot to mention. Mary and I will be serving a free Christmas Day dinner at the community center. If you have no other plans, you and Mikey are both more than welcome to come. I hope to see you both there."

Sarah thanks him and tells him they'll be there. Phillip says he looks forward to seeing her again, then turns back around and goes to his car. He opens the door for Mary before smiling one last time at Sarah, Mikey, and the neighbors. He then gets in the car, which heads off down the street.

CHAPTER 12

CHRISTMAS DAY DINNER

It's now Christmas Day. Phillip and Mary are standing outside the entrance of the community center, where a long line of people have gathered for the free Christmas community dinner being provided by the Phillip Bates Foundation.

Beside Phillip and Mary at the entrance is a police officer who's providing security for the event. He hands a bullhorn to Phillip, who addresses the crowd.

"OK, everyone, we're about to get started here. But before we open the doors, I wanted to say a few words. I just wanted to say that even though the turnout here today is far better than we'd expected, there's more than enough food for everyone. We really want everyone to have a great dinner, and we hope everyone is having a very Merry Christmas. Mary and I want to wish everyone the very best in the coming year."

The crowd applauds both of them, then Phillip turns to the people at the doors and tells them to go ahead and open them. He and Mary then head in first, followed by the people in the front of the line. As the auditorium fills with dozens of people, several other volunteers join the serving line to help serve the food.

Phillip and Mary make their way to the end of the line, handing out gifts to each person who comes through. The auditorium is very large and able to accommodate hundreds of people. A large, beautiful Christmas tree is in the corner, and it's lit up very nice.

Each person comes through the line and grabs a tray at the front. As they make their way through the line, they're given a Christmas day dinner, with a choice of chicken or ham, with mashed potatoes, corn or green beans, apple sauce or cranberry sauce or fruit, a dinner roll or cornbread, and a dessert of either apple pie or chocolate cake. After making their selections, each guest then moves to the end of the line, where Phillip and Mary wish them a Merry Christmas and Happy New Year and give them an envelope containing a $50 Walmart gift card. Various people Phillip has recently helped come through the line, and Sarah is the first person they recognize.

"Hello, Sarah and Mikey. And Merry Christmas to both of you," Phillip says.

Mary also greets them. "Hello. And Merry Christmas to both of you. I'm so glad you were able to make it here. And again, I'm so sorry for your loss. I hope Phillip and I were able to make things a little better for you?"

"Yes," Sarah says, "thank you both so much. I don't know where I'd be right now if it hadn't been for you. You really have saved my life."

Phillip responds, "You're welcome, Sarah. I'm glad we were able to help. Robert has told me you now have a nice apartment?"

Sarah says, "Yes, I do. I have a new apartment, and I was able to get some new clothes, too. Robert's helping me with the new house. He's very nice and very helpful."

"That's excellent news. Robert will keep me informed of the progress. If you have any problems, you be sure to call him," Phillip responds.

Sarah thanks them again, then moves out of line, allowing the next person to come through.

Pastor Jason Alexander comes through the line, and Mary tells him, "Pastor, how very wonderful it is to see you here today. I hope you're having a very Merry Christmas," then gives him a hug.

Phillip sees the pastor and tells him, "Merry Christmas" while shaking his hand.

Jason says, "Thank you both very much. I'm doing great. Thank you again for the money you gave last week to replace the gifts. We had a great turnout. Every child who showed up received a gift, and there were still several gifts left afterward that we gave to the Toys for Tots program."

Phillip responds, "You're very welcome. I'm glad I was able to help you. Any word yet on the suspects who stole the money?"

Jason says, "No, no information yet. But I got a good look at the suspect who was wearing the red hat, and I'm hopeful they'll catch them before anyone else gets robbed or hurt. I'm just so glad we were able to help these kids out. I never could have done it without your help."

Mary hands Jason an envelope with the Walmart gift card. He thanks them both, then moves out of line. A few other unknown customers come through the line next.

Dorothy Watts, from the Main Street Café car accident, comes through the line. Phillip sees her, says hello, and asks if she was able to get another car.

Dorothy says, "Yes, I was able to get another car. Thank you again, Mr. Bates. That was a really nice thing you did for me, and I'm very grateful."

Phillip tells her she's welcome, then introduces her to Mary, who says, "Hello. It's very nice to meet you. I hope you're having a Merry Christmas. Phillip told me about your car accident. I'm glad you weren't hurt."

Dorothy says, "Thank you. It's very nice to meet you, too. Yes, I was really very lucky, even though my car wasn't so lucky. Just when I thought everything was about to fall apart, your husband was right there, helping me out when I was desperate. He truly is a lifesaver."

Phillip says, "Well, I'm glad I just happened to be there when I was. Hopefully, that intersection will be safer for everyone soon. I'm having a stoplight placed there to make it easier for people to turn. It should be up in a week or so."

Dorothy says, "Oh, that is great news. That intersection has always been a really bad one."

She realizes she's holding up the line, so she tells Mary and Phillip thank you and wishes them both a Merry Christmas. Mary hands her one of the envelopes with a gift card as she exits the line.

A couple other people come through the line, then Charlene Jones comes by. Mary gives her an envelope with a gift card, then Charlene thanks her and Phillip, wishes them a Merry Christmas, and the exits the line.

Phillip and Mary look around and see the auditorium is now completely full of people enjoying their Christmas Day dinner.

CHAPTER 13

PHILLIP BATES INTERVIEW

Two weeks after Christmas, on January 5th, the newsroom at the TV station is about to play a selected part of their interview with Phillip Bates. Melissa Childs had interviewed him earlier. Although only part of the interview is being shown, she reports it will be shown in its entirety this coming evening.

Officer Mike Murphy is at home watching the afternoon news while working on his laptop. The interview clip begins as Melissa introduces herself and Phillip.

"Phillip, is it okay that I begin by giving our audience some background information on what you do?"

Phillip says, "Yes, that's fine."

"Now, the companies you own employ more people than any other employer in the state. You have several thousand people in this city alone working for you, and you make a lot of money from these companies. Yet unlike other wealthy people, you spend a lot more of your money helping others. You've built schools, parks, churches, homeless shelters, and no-kill animal shelters. You're building a local community college, currently under construction. You've also built hospitals and orphanages for children who have lost their parents. You've invested a lot of money in research for diseases. Your investment in this city is very large, and very generous. My question to you is, why do you do all this? Why do you spend so much money on these things, knowing they won't provide anything to you in return?"

Phillip stops Melissa right there. "Now wait a minute, Melissa. That's where you're wrong. I do what I do for several reasons. Yes, I do own a lot of businesses, and I do make a lot of money from them. Obviously, I no longer need to make more money. That's no longer my goal. In fact, that hasn't been my goal for a very long time. I'll never use the money I have, and there are a lot of other people out there who could use it to better their lives. I've made my money from my companies because they're successful, and my companies have been successful because my employees and customers have helped make them successful. So, the way I look at it, I'm simply giving back to the communities that have created such enormous wealth for me. I'm helping the same people who have helped me. You're wrong to say I don't get any return out of what I do. Look, when a young man or woman graduates from high school, if that individual goes to work and earns the federal or state minimum wage, they'll not only have a difficult life, they also won't be as productive as they might have been if they'd attended college. By going to college, they'll have a much better and happier life and be much more productive members of society. So, I feel when I help a young man or woman go to college, I'm making an investment in the community the same as I would by opening a business. Any business is only as good as its employees, and that's where my return comes in: Making these communities better by having better educated people living and working in them.

"Also, I really enjoy what I do. I enjoy using my money to make other people's dreams come true. I enjoy making people happy. When I see another person smiling and happy and that happiness is a direct result of my actions, it makes me feel better about myself. And that's very rewarding to me personally."

Melissa responds "I see. Now, I wanted to ask. You have a reputation for giving people money at various times, during holidays or emergencies that have come up. I've heard you've given money to people involved in traffic accidents, or maybe after the loss of loved ones or medical issues. Is this true?"

Phillip says, "Yes, you're correct. I do often help people spontaneously if I come upon a situation where I'm able to help. However, there have also been times where I wanted to help but was unable to. Either I didn't have any cash on me at the time or there might have been a security or safety concern. I rarely carry cash in person. It wouldn't be very wise to do that in my position. But sometimes my wife, Mary, or I might come upon a situation where cash can help and we do have the ability at that particular moment to help someone in need. In those situations, yes, we'll do what we can to help."

Mike is watching the interview with great interest, paying close attention. His eyes open wide when Phillip talks about how he or his wife might sometimes have cash on them.

Melissa says, "I understand. But why it is that you give so much money to people and organizations and do so many good things for so many people when others don't do the same thing? I see you as an exception among the top 1% of wealthiest people in the world. While you give so much away and do so much to help others, other people in similar positions, like Bill Gates, Warren Buffett, and Mark Zuckerberg don't give away money like you do. Why is it that you do it when they won't?"

Phillip says, "I'm not really sure how to answer that. All the other wealthy people I've encountered in my life don't feel the same way as I do when it comes to helping people. I've always looked at ways of using my money to help others, while other billionaires only look for ways to make more money they don't even need and will never use. People like Bill Gates, Warren Buffett, Mark Zuckerberg, Larry Page, and even Donald Trump don't do what I do because they don't feel the same way about helping the people as I do. To them, poor people are what they call 'peasants'. Bill Gates and Warren Buffett have a program they call the 'Giving Pledge', where they pledge to give away at least half of their wealth. But take a look at both of them. Both are still multi-billionaires, trying to do whatever they can to acquire even more money. They buy stocks and buy and sell and invest in companies. They aren't spending their days looking for ways to give their money away like they say they are, or like I am. And as far as the Bill and Melinda Gates foundation, it's a complete joke. They give money to hospitals and clinics, but the requirements to apply for a grant are so strict, it prevents most people from even bothering to apply. That foundation doesn't give money to individuals in desperate need like mine does. Both of them will die with billions of dollars still in their accounts. I can't answer as to what their motivation is. I can only answer what it is I'm trying to do. I enjoy helping people and feel it's my purpose in life now."

This small part of the full interview concludes, and Melissa, now in a live shot, says the interview can be seen in its entirety this evening at 6 PM. The news anchor then comes back on the air to repeat the hour's top news story.

"Police are looking for a suspect in the robbery and attempted carjacking of a senior citizen. The suspect is described as an African American male in his late teens or early twenties, about six feet tall and slender. He was last seen wearing a red baseball cap and blue jeans on Race Street. Anyone with any information regarding this case is urged to please call police immediately."

Mike Murphy, still watching the TV, has an angry look of disgust on his face when the description of the black suspect is announced. The news broadcast ends, and Mike takes the laptop off his lap and turns off the TV. He then gets up, heads toward the front door of the house, and leaves the house to go to the corner market.

As Mike comes out the front door of his house, his wife, Carol, is pulling into the driveway. She gets out of the car and asks him where he's going.

Mike says, "I'm just making a quick run down to the corner market. Do you need anything?"

Carol says, "From the liquor store? Uhh…no, I don't need anything from the liquor store. I have to get ready to go to Kim's baby shower."

Mike says, "It's not a liquor store. I'll see you later when you get home, then. Have fun."

Carol stops to ask him, "Hey, can we talk when you get home about that animal adoption event I saw on TV? They're waiving all the fees for anyone who adopts a cat or dog. Remember we talked about it before? But you never answered me. I wanted to go and see if maybe we can find a little dog to adopt."

Mike says, "Sure. We'll talk about it when I get home in a little while."

Carol says, "OK. I'll see you soon. Be safe. I love you."

She gives him a goodbye kiss, then goes in the house as Mike gets in his car and drives off towards the market.

CHAPTER 14

WALT'S MARKET ROBBERY

Walt's Market is a small neighborhood market that sells alcohol and a limited selection of groceries, similar to a Circle K or 7-11. It's been in business for several years, and Walt Meyers, who's Caucasian, is the owner.

Mike is a regular customer of the store, as it's the closest store to his house. He pulls into the parking lot and goes inside the store. As he enters, he sees Walt at the counter, finishing a sale to a black customer.

As the customer walks towards the front door to exit the store after making his purchase, he passes Mike, who's just come in the door. Mike walks around the customer and deliberately doesn't hold the door open for him. The customer, now behind Mike, turns around and has a look on his face indicating he thought that was pretty rude of Mike. Walter sees this and doesn't appear very happy with Mike but still greets him anyway.

"Hey Mike, how's it going?" Walt asks.

Without even looking at Walt, Mike says, "Ahh, same shit, different day," then heads towards the back of the store to look for some items.

As Mike shops, he hears the sound of bells jingle, indicating someone entering the front door of the market. He turns to see a black man who's apparently come in to rob the store. The man appears young, in his early to mid-twenties. He isn't wearing a mask; just sunglasses and a black ski cap. Holding a pistol, the man quickly makes his way towards Walt at the cash register, then orders him to give him the money in the register while pointing his gun directly at him.

"Give me your fucking money, motherfucker – NOW!" the robber yells at Walt.

Walt says, "OK, man, don't shoot."

Walt pushes the silent alarm button with his knee down below the counter, then turns to look up at the security camera in the corner. Seeing him looking up at the camera, the robber looks up to see what Walt was looking at, which gives the camera a good picture of his face.

On patrol by himself at the moment about 10 miles away, Mike's partner, Brian, hears the call come over the radio.

"All units, 211 in progress. Walt's Market, 4th Street and Highland Avenue. Silent alarm triggered."

Brian responds to the call. "Unit 32 to base. Responding to 211 in progress at Walt's Market, 4th Street and Highland Avenue."

Inside the market, as Walt starts to hit buttons on the cash register to open it, the robber hears the sound of rapid footsteps coming behind him, as if someone's quickly approaching. He turns around to see Mike running quickly towards him, and before he can react, Mike punches him in the face so hard, he's instantly knocked off his feet and falls to the ground, dropping his pistol on the ground. Mike's punch is so hard, it breaks the robber's sunglasses.

Even though the robber is now disarmed and only semi-conscious on the ground, Mike grabs his shirt and repeatedly punches him in the face while screaming racial insults at him. "You motherfuckin' nigger piece of shit! You're gonna come in here and rob this store while I'm in here?" Mike keeps screaming at him while continuing to punch him in the face. "Well, FUCK YOU, NIGGER!" he screams.

Walt yells to Mike, "That's enough!" But Mike doesn't respond, so Walt yells even louder and more firmly, "MIKE, THAT'S ENOUGH!"

Mike stops his assault on the robber and looks up at Walt, who appears completely shocked at what he's done to the guy. Mike lets go of the robber's shirt, and the man drops back down to the floor, bloody and appearing lifeless. Mike then goes over and picks up the robber's gun off the floor and tells Walt to give him the phone.

Walt tells Mike he'd already hit the alarm and the police were on the way. Hearing police sirens approaching in the distance, Mike briefly looks toward the front door, then back at Walt and notices the security camera behind Walt, pointed directly towards him.

He asks, "Is that camera working?"

"Yes, it works," Walt responds.

"Where's the tape?"

"It's in the machine in the back room."

"Go get the tape."

Walt heads towards the back room to retrieve the tape. While he's in the back, Mike hears the robber coughing and looks down to see him coughing up blood. He forcefully turns the robber over, grabs his hands, and puts handcuffs on him, then turns him back over. The robber is now looking directly at Mike, who yells at him, making more racially sensitive statements.

"Was it worth it? Huh? You fucking little punk-ass niggers never learn, do you? Was it worth it, you fucking monkey?" He then reads the robber his own version of the robber's rights. "You're under arrest. You have the right to shut the fuck up. If you give up this right, I'll shut your black ass up. You have the right to an attorney. And since your worthless black ass can't afford an attorney, we'll provide a really fucked up one for you that'll make sure you land in prison."

The robber just looks at Mike without saying anything. He appears to be in shock or has maybe suffered a concussion. The blood pouring out of his nose indicates he probably has a broken nose.

Walt comes back up front with a DVD after about a minute and gives it to Mike, who tells Walt he'll have this "piece of shit" out of here in no time.

Mike looks at Walt and says, "Hey, he tried to resist. That's why I beat his ass. He tried to go for his gun, even after I hit him. You didn't hear me talking trash to him, and this DVD doesn't exist. That camera isn't working. Are we clear here?"

Walt hesitates, then says, "But Mike –"

Mike yells in a firm tone, "ARE WE CLEAR?!"

Walt says, "Yeah, man…we're clear," looking very scared.

After about 2 minutes, a police car pulls up outside the market, then a second car pulls up. Mike sees out the window police officers from both cars have exited their vehicles.

One of the officers lifts a bullhorn and yells, "Alright, we have the store surrounded. Come out with your hands up!"

Mike tells Walt just to wait inside the store as he puts up his hands and exits the front door to go outside.

The officers outside are behind their cars now, with their guns drawn at seeing a suspect coming out of the store.

Mike yells out to them, "It's alright. I'm officer Mike Murphy. I have the suspect in custody inside the store."

The officers recognize Mike, lower their weapons, and head towards him as another officer calls off any further assistance. When they arrive at the front door, Mike leads two other officers into the store. Inside, the two officers go over to the suspect, see he's all beat to hell, and make sure he's okay. They notice he looks very weak and appears to need medical attention.

One of the officers asks him, "Hey man, are you okay? We have an ambulance on the way, okay?"

The suspect looks at the officer and just nods. After that, he falls over. The officer helps lift him up, trying to keep him awake while he calls for an ambulance.

Another police car comes into the parking lot and parks. Brian gets out of the car and walks over to an officer to find out what happened.

The officer tells him, "Hey, your partner just happened to be here when some little punk came into the store to rob it. Mike took him down, and it looks like he took him down pretty hard from the looks of the kid."

Brian asks if Mike's still inside. The officer says he is, so Brian heads inside and walks over to Mike.

He tells him, "Hey, I was on patrol and heard the call over the radio. I heard you were involved. What happened?"

Mike says, "I was getting something to make lunch, and this punk came in, trying to rob the place. I was able to disarm him, but he tried to resist when I identified myself as a police officer and told him he was under arrest. So, I had to restrain him to get him in custody."

Brian looks down at the kid, then back to Mike. "*That's* restraining him? You had to do *that* to him?" he asks.

"Hey, he tried to go for his gun, even after I got it out of his hands. I didn't have a choice here, man. Ask him, he saw it," Mike says, pointing to Walt.

Brian looks at Walt and asks him if it really happened the way Mike described. His tone indicates he doesn't really believe Mike's explanation.

Walt looks at Mike, who's giving him a mean look to try to scare him into agreeing with his explanation. He's afraid of Mike, and it shows on his face when he answers Brian.

"Yeah. Yeah, that's what happened," Walt says.

Brian looks at Walt, then back at Mike. He knows Walt and Mike are both lying.

An ambulance has now pulled into the parking lot, and the suspect is soon loaded into the ambulance on a gurney. The ambulance then heads for the hospital, with a police car following it, leaving the only remaining police car in the parking lot belonging to Brian.

Mike is still inside, talking to Walt. He warns him again, saying, "Remember what I said. You didn't see or hear shit. All you heard was him telling you to give him the money. And this (holding the video disc) doesn't exist. The security camera wasn't working."

Walt just looks at Mike, who's giving him a mean look. After a few moments, he says, "I didn't see anything."

Mike nods to him, then leaves the store and goes out to Brian, who's standing by his car.

Brian asks, "So what really happened here, Mike?"

Mike says, "That little punk nigger came in to rob the place while I was there. I was in the back of the store and heard him come in, and he pointed a gun at Walt and demanded money. I just ran up and smashed him. He dropped the gun, then I pounded his ass."

Brian asks, "Why did you do that? Was he still trying to fight?"

Mike says, "Hell no. I dropped him. He was pretty much out of it."

Brian asks, "Then why did you keep hitting him?"

Mike says, "Because I'm havin' a real bad day. I just saw that shit on TV about that nigger with the red baseball cap who robbed that old lady and tried to jack her car – and I bet it's the same punk who ripped off the church, too. And then I come in here and see this shit. I mean, what the fuck? I'm just sick and tired of these worthless fuckin' niggers doin' this shit."

Brian asks Mike about Walt inside the store, and Mike tells him Walt isn't going to say anything because he'd already given him a warning. Brian then tells Mike he noticed a camera inside the store and asks him about it, as well as if there were any additional witnesses.

Mike says, "Yeah, there was a camera. But I got the disc and told Walt to say the camera was broken. And there wasn't anyone else in the store."

Brian says, "Okay. I'll write up the report then to indicate the security camera system wasn't working. Give me a minute while I go inside to talk to Walt." He enters the store, comes up to Walt, and asks, "Walt, I need to know. Was the story Mike gave me earlier what really happened? And does that camera really not work?"

Walt pauses for a moment before saying, "Yes, his story is true, and the camera doesn't work."

Brian responds with a threat. "OK, the camera better *not* have been working. And you better *not* have seen anything, because that mean son of a bitch out there by my car is my partner. He told me what really happened in here. And yeah, he beat that guy because he was a black piece of crap. But he also saved your ass. Now, I'm pretty sure you don't want me or him coming back in here looking for you, right? I mean, you seem like a pretty simple guy, Walt. I'd hate for your life to get really complicated. That just wouldn't turn out very good for you. You understand what I'm saying to you, Walt?"

Walt nods and tells Brian he understands. Brian then tells him to have a good day before leaving the store. Back outside, Brian resumes talking to Mike, then they both turn to see Walt standing by the front door, looking out at them. A few moments later, they get in their cars and leave the parking lot.

* * *

Later that evening, Mike and Brian are in Captain Williams's office, getting another warning about the event at Walt's Market.

"I'm just telling you both, this better have gone down exactly the way your report shows it, Officer Davis," Williams looks at Mike, "because you beat this kid so bad, he fell into a coma a couple hours ago. The fact that your report goes along with the statement by the store owner is what's keeping you both out of trouble." He pauses, then continues. "And just for your information, Phillip Bates has been made aware of this incident. He also heard about your prior arrest incident, where you pulled over to beat the crap out of that other black suspect who was in handcuffs in the back of your car."

Mike doesn't understand why that's relevant. "So what? What the hell does Phillip Bates have to do with anything? Who gives a shit what he thinks?" he asks.

Williams says, "Phillip Bates sits in on all the city council meetings. He's best friends with the mayor, and a personal friend of mine, too. And his foundation also contributes over one million dollars a month to this department alone, which means he's paying my salary, and yours, too. If he tells the mayor to terminate you two, you'll both be out of here in a heartbeat." He turns to Mike. "And your actions, Mike, are really starting to piss him off. If I find out there's anything about this report that isn't true or any other evidence turns up showing this report isn't a hundred percent accurate, you'll both be outta here immediately. I hope that's clear."

Mike says he understands, then Williams tells them they're both dismissed and orders them to get out of his office.

As they're leaving the police station, Brian asks, "Mike, what the hell were you thinking? Why the hell did you beat that kid so bad? You went way too far, because that kid's in a coma now."

Mike snaps, "Well, good! Maybe these little punks will learn to stop screwing around, then. What the hell is wrong with you, Brian? I'm not the one who went in there to rob the place. What the hell do you think would have happened if I hadn't been there? That kid wasn't wearing a mask. That guy running the place, Walt, would probably be dead right now. What the hell are you getting on *my* case for?"

Brian says, "You don't know that Walt would be dead, and you wouldn't have beat that kid as bad as you did if he wasn't black. Look, you know I don't like these scumbags either, but you really gotta stop all this racial bullshit, or we're both gonna get screwed, man. We've been warned twice now by the captain. If he saw the video of that crap and me covering for you, we'd both be out of a job, and you might even be in jail. I think the captain is just looking for a reason to bust our asses after that last warning, especially if this Bates guy is putting pressure on him. Don't give him a reason to fire us, man."

Mike says, "The captain isn't gonna fire us, and there isn't any video anymore, because I took the disc from the camera system. And fuck Bates. That kid was a piece of trash. Did you see his rap sheet? He's been arrested over twenty times and has been to prison twice. This city is better off without a piece of garbage like that."

Brian tells him it isn't for them to decide what's best for the city, to which Mike responds maybe it needs to be up to them to make that decision.

They both get in their car and leave the station.

CHAPTER 15

ANIMAL ADOPTION DAY

Mike and Carol Murphy are pulling into the parking lot of an animal adoption event at the Humane Society. The parking lot is full because all adoptions are free, as Phillip Bates and his wife, Mary, are paying the adoption and registration fees for all animals.

Mike and Carol get out of their car and head towards the front door of the center and go inside. While on their way in, Mike notices a Lexus in the parking lot, with the license plate "MBATES1". As Mike and Carol enter, they approach the table near the front, and a customer service employee welcomes them to the center.

"Hi. How can I help you today?" the young lady asks.

Carol responds, "Hi. We'd like to take a look at the dogs you have available for adoption. We heard there were free adoptions going on today. What do we need to do?"

"That's correct," the young lady says. "Well, they aren't free. Mr. Phillip Bates is here today. He and his wife are paying the fees for all adoptions today. You won't have to pay any adoption or registration fees today, and we're even including a free chip implant in case your pet is ever lost."

"Oh, well that's really nice of him," Carol says.

Mike hears the woman say Phillips's name and recognizes it. "Wait. Did you say Phillip Bates?" he asks.

"Yes, that's him over there. You'll be able to meet him before you leave."

Carol responds, "Yes, definitely. I've heard a lot about him."

Mike, staring at Phillip, says, "Yeah, I've heard a lot about him, too. I look forward to meeting him."

Carol asks the woman what they need to do, and she gives them a card, pencil, and instructions to write down the number on the cage of any dog or cat they're interested in. Carol and Mike then walk toward the back area, where the dogs are located. Mike shoots Phillip an angry look as he and Carol pass him along the way, then the two of them start looking at various dogs in their cages, making observations about each one.

Carol: "Too mean looking."

Mike: "Too ugly."

Carol: "Too big."

Mike: "Too messy."

Carol: "Too hairy."

Mike: "Too wasted. He looks drunk."

Carol: "Too crazy."

Mike and Carol then come upon a cage with a small gold-colored short-haired Chihuahua with a tail that curves up.

Mike says, "Too small."

Carol says, "Wait. He's not too small. He's cute."

Mike says, "Not too small? He's a rodent!" He looks directly at the dog and says, "Yo quiero Taco Bell."

Carol snaps, "He's not Taco Bell. He's so cute."

Mike says, "I'm gonna end up stepping on him. I won't even see him."

Ignoring him, Carol says, "I wanna take him outside."

Mike responds, "Fine. I thought we were getting a dog here, not a rat?"

Carol snaps, "He's *not* a rat!"

She and Mike return to the front, where she asks the employee if they can take the dog outside. The employee gets a leash for the dog, takes it outside for Mike and Carol to spend time with, then goes back inside, telling them she'll be back in about 10 minutes. Carol thanks her, then watches as the dog starts running around all over the place right as the employee heads back inside the building.

She says, "I think he's absolutely adorable. I'd like to get him. What do you think?"

Mike responds, "I just think he's a little bit too small. Not exactly what I was thinking when you suggested getting a dog. I don't know."

The dog continues to run around for a while, then Mike picks up a small rubber ball off the ground and throws it for the dog to fetch. The dog goes and gets the ball, brings it right up to Mike, drops it at his feet, then starts jumping up at him, wanting to be picked up. Mike reaches down to pick up the dog, who's excited and wagging his tail fast. As Mike brings the dog up near his face, it starts licking him, showing a lot of excitement and happiness. This makes Mike change his mind about the dog, and he breaks out into a smile.

"OK, I'm sold. We'll take him," Mike says.

Carol claps her hands in excitement. "Yay! Thank you, honey," she says, hugging him.

The employee comes back out to check on the dog. "So, how are we doing out here? Do you folks have any questions?"

Mike responds, "Nah, I think we're good here. We'll take this one."

The employee responds, "Oh, okay, great. Well, come on inside, and we can get the paperwork started for him."

All three of them head back inside the building, then Mike and Carol enter the front lobby with the card they were given to fill out earlier and get in a line to get the paperwork started. As they're waiting in line, Mike sees Phillip Bates again; he's talking to another customer, with Mary Bates right next to him. Mike just stares at him, with a less than friendly look on his face. He also notices around Mary's neck what appears to be a very expensive necklace.

The customer in front of Mike and Carol finishes up with the employee, then they sit down in front of her and give her the card they filled out.

"Hello. How can I help you?" she asks.

Carol responds, "Hello. We want him! He's so cute."

She hands the employee the card. The specialist takes it, then puts the kennel number into her computer to pull up the information.

"OK, this dog is a one-year-old male Chihuahua. He was given up by his owner, who was an older lady unable to care for him anymore. We actually just got him in this morning."

Carol says, "This morning? Really?"

As Carol and the service lady are talking, Mike, sitting next to Carol, keeps looking over at Phillip Bates.

The adoption specialist says, "Yeah. Typically, smaller dogs like this tend to go pretty quickly. Usually, families with small kids like these kinds of dogs because they feel safer having their kids around a small dog, rather than a bigger dog. Do you have your ID with you?"

Carol says, "Yes" and gets out her ID.

The adoption specialist enters Carol's information into the computer, asking, "Is all the information on here correct?"

Carol responds, saying the information is correct. The specialist then asks for Carol's phone number.

"Yes, 555-867-5309," Carol tells her.

"OK. Any idea what you'd like to name the dog?"

Carol says, "Yes, his name is going to be Clark."

Michael says, "Clark? Where did that name come from?"

Carol responds, "From watching Smallville of course! You should know that. I'm naming him after Clark Kent!"

Michael rolls his eyes. "Uhh, okay. Clark."

"Oh, get over it. He's so cute!" she says, with an excited smile.

The adoption specialist says, "OK, Clark Murphy it is. Now, there aren't going to be any fees; however, you'll have to come back in the next couple of days to pick up the dog. We'll contact you when you can come pick him up."

Carol asks, "Awww, we can't take him with us now?"

Mike still keeps looking over at Phillip Bates while sitting next to Carol. He seems more interested in Bates than he is in the adoption process. When Bates glances over and notices Mike looking at him, Mike quickly looks away, back toward the adoption specialist.

"No, he has to be given his shots, then he'll have surgery to be neutered. All animal adoptions are either spayed or neutered. How would you like us to contact you when he's ready to be picked up?"

Carol responds, "A phone call will be fine to the number I gave you, 555-867-5309."

The specialist responds, "OK, we'll contact you when he's ready. It'll probably be 2 to 3 days. Here's the paperwork for him. You'll also be given a leash and medication for him for his surgery when you come pick him up."

Carol responds. "OK. Well, thank you very much."

Mike and Carol stand up, and the specialist shakes Carol's hand, then Mike's. "You're welcome. And thank you for coming in. Mr. Phillip Bates would also like to thank you. He's right over there."

Michael responds, "Thank you," then both of them head over to another table, where Phillip and Mary have both just finished talking with another customer.

Phillip greets them. "Hello. I'm Phillip Bates, and this is my wife, Mary. And who might you be?"

Carol responds, "Hello. It's very nice to meet you in person. I've heard so much about you from news reports. My name is Carol, and this is my husband, Michael."

Phillip shakes hands with both Michael and Carol, then Mary shakes their hands as well.

Carol says, "I also wanted to say thank you for this today. We probably wouldn't have come and adopted a dog if it hadn't been for you."

Phillip responds, "Well, you're very welcome. What kind of dog did you get today?"

Carol says, "We got a little Chihuahua. He's really very cute. I can't wait to take him home."

Phillip says, "Well, that's really nice. I sure hope you enjoy the dog. I love animals myself, and I just hate seeing them sit in these cages – or even worse, being put down because nobody wants them. It's just really sad. And I just think it's great when folks like you come down to help these animals out and give them new homes. Thank you for adopting the dog. You probably saved its life today."

Carol says, "Well, you're the one who made it happen. Thank you both again. It was really nice to meet both of you."

She shakes hands with both Phillip and Mary again. Phillip then extends his hand to shake Mike's hand again. Right then, the adoption specialist calls out to Mary, having forgotten something.

"Mrs. Murphy?"

They all look at the specialist.

"We forgot to give you this picture of your dog."

Phillip says, "Carol Murphy? Mike Murphy? Police Officer Mike Murphy?"

Mike grabs Phillip's hand, which is still extended to shake his own. He then says, "Yes, I'm Police Officer Mike Murphy. And I hear you've been having words with my captain, Jon Williams?"

Phillip responds, "Actually, I had words with your chief of police, Dan Brady, because I hear there have been complaints about you, involving incidents of excessive use of force against minority individuals. That's something we don't need and don't condone in this city, Mr. Murphy." He speaks in a firm, strong tone, indicating he doesn't back down or let anyone intimidate him, as Mike appears to be trying to do.

Mike moves in closer to Phillip while still firmly holding his hand, even pulling Phillip's hand toward him.

He says, "You know, any time anyone, ANYONE, threatens me or my partner or my family or friends, I will ALWAYS use whatever force I feel is necessary to remove that threat. You might just do well to keep that in mind in the future, Mr. Bates."

Still holding Phillip's hand, Mike pulls back a little bit. Phillip pauses for a moment, then moves in closer to Mike, pulling his hand towards himself just a little.

Phillip says, "You know, I donate about seventy percent of the budget for your police department. So, seventy percent of your paycheck comes from me. I have enormous influence in the city council and police department here, which means I have the power to have an officer removed from the force any time I choose. You might just do well to keep that in mind in the future, Mr. Murphy."

Phillip then pulls back a little bit, forcefully grabs Mike's hand with his other hand, and rips it away from his own hand. Staring right into Mike's eyes with a very firm, almost angry, look on his face, he says, "Good day to you, sir."

Mike gives Phillip a blank stare when he sees he isn't backing down. Meanwhile, Mary and Carol have confused looks on their faces because they don't understand what's going on between the two men.

After a few tense moments, Mike says, "Come on, honey, let's go," then grabs Carol's hand and heads for the exit.

Phillip and Mike give each other one final look before Mike and Carol head out the front door.

Once they're gone, Mary asks Phillip, "What was that all about?"

Phillip responds, "That guy is a cop, and he's a racist piece of crap. I had to give the police chief a warning about him. You stay clear of that guy, okay?"

Mary just shakes her head in agreement and says, "OK."

CHAPTER 16

BUBBA WILSON

Back in the police station parking lot that evening, Mike and Brian are pulling out of the station driveway.

Brian says, "Hopefully, tonight will be a quiet one, huh?"

Mike responds. "I doubt it. It's a full moon. It always seems to bring out the nutcases."

Brian says, "Yeah, that's true."

Bubba Wilson is a mildly retarded black male. He's visiting a friend, Trey Johnson, when his mom calls and says it's time to come home. Wearing blue jeans and having a red baseball cap, Bubba's appearance is similar to that of the suspect in several previous crimes in the city. He is over 6 feet tall, and slender.

Trey's mother, Miss Johnson, takes the call, then tells Bubba, "Bubba, your mom just called. She says it's time for you to come home now. Your dinner is about ready."

Bubba responds, "OK, Miss Johnson. Can I come back tomorrow?"

"It's okay with me as long as it's okay with your mama. I'll see you later, Bubba. Don't forget to take your game back home with you."

Bubba says, "OK. Thank you, Mrs. Johnson."

Trey tells Bubba, "See ya later, Bubba."

Bubba responds, "Bye, Trey. Goodbye, Miss Johnson."

Miss Johnson says, "Goodnight, Bubba. You be careful goin' home."

Bubba grabs his red baseball cap next to him on the couch and his video game, which is in a hard, black plastic DVD style case. He leaves the apartment carrying the DVD in his hand.

Mike and Brian are on patrol when a call comes out for the same suspect in previous crimes trying to break into a car.

"All units, 504 in progress. 510 Highland Ave. Woman calling in, reporting a person is trying to break into her car. Suspect is described as a black male, early 20s, approximately 6 feet tall, wearing blue jeans and a red baseball cap."

Mike tells Brian, "Man, I've had it with this shit. Let's finally nail this son of a bitch right now."

Brian responds, "Hell yeah."

Mike calls in that they're responding to the 504 as their car speeds off to the call. The suspect is still attempting to break into the car a few minutes later when he looks up and sees their patrol car pulling up in the street with its lights on. He's on the other side of the lot, where he'd been trying to break into the car.

Mike says, "There's that little punk right there. Let me out here. Go around to the other side of the block and cut him off."

Brian responds, "I'm on it."

Mike gets out of the car to chase the suspect on foot, while Brian continues driving down the road to try to catch him on the other side of the alley. Seeing Mike get out of the car, the suspect takes off running down an alley near it. Mike can't see down the alley because he's coming towards it at an angle. The alley has other cross streets or alleys where people could be coming or going.

As the suspect comes up to a cross street, he turns one way and runs down the street towards the location where Brian was driving. At the same time, from the other direction, Bubba comes walking out from around the street into the alley, unaware of what's going on and that Mike is about to come running into the alley, chasing the suspect, who has the same appearance and similar baseball cap to what he's wearing.

As Mike enters the alley, he sees Bubba and assumes he's the suspect he's after. So, he immediately draws his firearm and orders Bubba to freeze, pointing his gun at him.

Mike says, "Freeze! Right there! Don't fuckin move!"

Bubba is startled, as he doesn't know what's going on or why Mike has his gun pointed at him. The video game is in Bubba's hand, and he's holding it in such a way that it's hanging down from his hand in a vertical position. An alley street light is reflecting on the spine of the case, making it appear long and metallic, like a handgun. Startled and caught off guard, Bubba raises his hands in the air, and in the process his hand holding the game case comes up, pointing towards Mike.

Bubba says, "Wait."

Mike fires his handgun twice, hitting Bubba in the chest both times. Bubba drops the game and immediately falls to the ground.

Mike then runs up to him, still pointing his gun at Bubba. As he gets within a couple of feet of Bubba, he realizes he was holding a DVD case, not a gun. Bubba is still alive but dying as he looks up at Mike with tears coming out of his eyes and blood flowing out of his mouth.

While shaking, Bubba asks Mike, "Why did you shoot me, Mr. Police Officer?"

Realizing he shot the wrong suspect, Mike kneels down to Bubba and says, "Come on, kid. Hang in there. I'm getting an ambulance for you."

Bubba says his final words. "I'm sorry, Mr. Officer. I'm cold." He then loses consciousness.

Mike realizes he's in trouble and looks around; seeing no one around yet, he pulls a small handgun out of his ankle holster and places it in Bubba's hand. He then picks up the DVD case and throws it like a Frisbee behind him as far as he can. As he hears someone coming from down the alley where the suspect had run, he quickly stands up, backs up a couple feet, and points his gun at the now deceased Bubba.

Brian comes running from around the corner with his gun drawn and sees Murphy with his gun pointed at Bubba.

He yells, "What happened?"

Mike responds, "I got the son of a bitch. I told him to freeze, and he pulled a gun on me. I had to take him down. We got him, man."

Brian says, "Mike, I got the guy around the corner who was breaking into the car. This isn't him. I've got the guy in custody in the back of my car right now."

A look of shock dawns on Mike's face as he realizes he's really screwed up and just killed an innocent, unarmed black man.

He says, "Well, this kid pulled a gun on me. I don't know what the hell he was thinking, but I didn't have a choice when I saw that gun pointed at me."

As Brian and Mike stare at each other, Brian suspects Mike is lying to him again.

Several police cars arrive, and other officers join them at the scene. Bubba is soon covered on a gurney and loaded into an ambulance as detectives join the scene.

Captain Williams says to Mike, "Alright Mike, you know the drill here. You're being taken off the street and will be on desk duty pending the outcome of an investigation into this shooting."

Mike responds, "Yes, Captain."

Williams says, "Go on, now. Get outta here. Go home, Murphy."

Mike and Brian get into their car and drive off, leaving the scene.

* * *

At home, Mike watches news reports of the shooting as Bubba's relatives and friends are interviewed. He's drinking a beer and has a couple of empty beer cans on the coffee table in front of him. Melissa Childs is reporting on the TV.

"As you can see, there are many protesters out here continuing to demand justice for Bubba Wilson. They're demanding that Officer Mike Murphy be fired and charged with murder for the shooting. I'm here now with Miss Olivia Johnson, who's a friend of the family of Bubba Wilson and was with him about 5 minutes prior to this shooting. Miss Johnson, can you tell us what happened when you last saw Bubba before he left your apartment?"

Olivia responds, "Yeah. Bubba was over playing the video game with my son Trey. He comes over all the time, almost every day to play with my son. They were finishing up a game, and Bubba's mom called and said it was almost time for dinner and he had to come home. He asked if he could come back tomorrow, and I said it was okay by me if it was okay with his mom. And I told him not to forget to take his video game home he'd brought. He said goodbye to me and my son, and that was the last we ever saw him again."

Melissa continues. "So, you're saying he had a video game? We're being told the officer who shot Bubba ordered him to put his hands up and Bubba pointed a handgun he was carrying at the officer."

Olivia angrily responds, "What handgun? Bubba was mentally handicapped. He ain't never touched a gun in his life and wouldn't have even known how to use it, even if it was handed to him. He was a good boy. This officer is lying. He planted that gun on that boy. This officer was white, and Bubba was black, and that's why he's dead."

Melissa asks, "Are you saying you think this shooting was racially motivated?"

Olivia firmly responds, "Absolutely. If that boy had been white, he'd still be alive today. That officer needs to be in jail for the rest of his life for what he's done."

Mike turns off the TV as Carol comes in from the bedroom to try to help comfort him, but he becomes very mean and rejects her.

She says, "Mike, do you feel like talking about it?"

Pretty much drunk and not in a talking mood, Mike responds, "No, I don't want to talk about it. I just want to be left alone right now."

Carol says, "OK. Well, let me know if you change your mind. I'm here for you, honey."

Mike looks up at her and gives her a look like he's irritated with her. She turns around and walks away.

* * *

The next morning, empty beer cans are on the coffee table next to Carol's closed laptop. She's in the kitchen as Mike comes into the living room from the hallway, and she comes out to see him off as he's leaving for work.

Carol says, "I hope you have a good day, honey."

Mike responds, "Thanks. Hey, sorry about last night. I've just got a lot on my mind now with this investigation going on. I wasn't mad at you at all."

Carol gives him a hug, then says, "I know you've got a lot on your plate right now. Things will get better soon. Just give it some time."

Mike responds, "I know they will. OK, well I have to go. I'll see you after work."

Carol says, "OK, be safe. Oh, also, I wanted to ask about ordering that little gate for Clark so we can keep him off the carpet like we talked about?"

Mike says, "Oh, yeah. That's fine. Go ahead and order it. OK, I'll see you later tonight."

As he leaves out the front door, Carol starts to clean up the living room, picking up the beer cans and taking them to the trash can in the kitchen.

* * *

Mike walks into the police station, where several officers appear to be giving him the benefit of the doubt at the moment. Some of them just look at him, while others tell him they're sorry about what's happened. Captain Williams calls to Mike to come into his office, saying, "Murphy, I gotta talk to ya."

Mike goes into Williams's office, where he sees him sitting in his chair.

Williams says, "Close the door, Mike. Take a seat."

Mike sits down and asks, "What's up, Captain?"

Jon says, "I need to inform you that Internal Affairs is launching an investigation into this shooting. It's come to light that this kid you shot was mentally retarded, had never had any trouble with the police, and had good grades in school. And his friends are saying he was carrying a video game. That video game was discovered about 50 feet away from this kid on the ground, and it was in front of where he was walking. He had no warrants and wasn't in any trouble and would have had absolutely no reason to point a gun at a police officer. But you claim he pointed a gun at you, and you had to shoot him. Internal Affairs is now getting involved because the gun that was found in that kid's hand was the same gun reported stolen from our own property room last year. Now, I need a straight answer out of you right now, Mike." He pauses and looks directly at Mike. "Did you plant that gun on this kid?"

Mike responds, "No, I did not. I ran into the alley, chasing the suspect, and that kid was in the alley and looked exactly like the suspect I was chasing. I pointed my firearm at him and ordered him to freeze, and he pointed a gun towards me he had in his hand. So, I opened fire to defend myself."

Williams says, "I understand the suspect you were chasing, who was wanted for a number of crimes, had actually already been apprehended around the corner by your partner?"

Mike says, "Yes."

Williams asks, "What possible reason would there have been for this kid to be carrying a gun?"

Mike says, "I have no idea. I can't answer what the suspect was thinking or why he was carrying a gun."

Jon says, "Mike, you better be straight with me here. If you tell me now you planted that gun on that kid, you'll be terminated immediately, but I'll do the best I can to help keep any charges at a minimum. But if I find out later you lied to me, you'll be terminated *and* prosecuted to the fullest extent of the law, and I'll do *everything* I can to help push for the maximum. Do you understand that?"

Mike responds, "Yes, sir. I'm not lying. I told you exactly as it happened."

Williams now delivers the bad news. "Okay. Now on another note, I'm letting you know you'll now be assigned to permanent desk duty until further notice, regardless of the outcome of this investigation. You won't be out on the street anymore."

Appearing very angry, Mike says, "What? What the hell is this? Why not?"

Williams says, "Because about 70 percent of the budget for this department comes from the Phillip Bates Foundation." A look of extreme anger flashes over Mike's face and eyes as Jon continues. "We need that money for the budget, and after this incident, Bates has demanded that you be taken off the street. If we don't, he says he'll terminate any further funding towards our budget. Now, I've spoken with the mayor and chief about this, and they both agree that for the good of the department – and the community, with all the tension and protests going on – for the time being we have to take you off the street. Maybe later we can get you back out there, but for now we feel this is the best course of action."

Mike just stares at Williams for a few moments, with an angry look on his face. He then says, "OK. Is that it?"

Williams says, "Yup. That's it for now. Report to the desk sergeant out there. He has a desk assignment ready for you."

Mike gets up and is headed toward the door when Williams calls him.

"Mike?"

Mike turns around.

Williams says, "I'm sorry, man. I'm sorry this happened."

Mike says, "Me, too, Captain!" He then leaves the office.

* * *

Back at Mike's house, Carol is in the living room, which she's just finished cleaning. She sits down on the couch to take a break, grabs the laptop off the coffee table, and opens it to order the gate for her dog. She clicks on the browser icon to open it and is directed to a default Google search page. When she clicks on the URL line to type in the website she wants to go to, the browsing history drops down. One of the entries in the history is www.mightyplace.com – Michael Murphy. Carol doesn't recognize the website and wonders what it is, so she clicks on the link. The page that comes up is a complete profile, including several pictures of Mike with another woman. His arm is around her in one of the pictures, and he's kissing her in another one.

Completely shocked, Carol puts her hand over her mouth like she's about to throw up. She then sees a link for pictures, clicks on it, and is taken to a picture gallery with dozens of other pictures of Mike and this woman spending time together. Carol has tears coming out of her eyes now. She sets the laptop back down on the coffee table, gets up, and goes into the hallway towards her bedroom.

* * *

Back at the station, Mike is walking down a hallway, while Brian is coming towards him, then stops him in the hall.

Brian asks, "Hey Mike, what's going on?"

Mike says, "I'm off patrol and on permanent desk duty for now, even after these investigations. That's what's going on."

Brian asks, "What? Why?"

Mike says, "Because that fucker, Phillip Bates, told the chief either to take me off or he wasn't gonna give any more money to the department."

Brian says, "Oh man, that sucks, dude. What are you gonna do now?"

Mike says, "What can I do? I guess I'm stuck shining a seat with my ass. Man, I better not run into him on the street alone any time soon, or his ass is toast."

Brian says, "Well, that just sucks. I'm sorry to hear it, buddy. I gotta get going though. They assigned some new kid with me. I gotta go show him the ropes. We'll talk later, okay man?"

Surprised, Mike asks, "They assigned you a new partner?"

Brian responds, "Yeah. I was kinda surprised. I guess I know why now though. I gotta run."

Mike wishes Brian good luck, but inside he's absolutely furious at what's happened to him.

* * *

Arriving home from work, Mike enters through the front door and sees all the lights in the house are out and Carol isn't there to greet him as usual. The only light he notices is from the laptop computer sitting on the coffee table. It's aimed so the screen can be easily seen by anyone coming in the front door. On the screen is a picture from the Mighty Place website, with Mike with his arms around another woman, kissing her. On the mousepad of the laptop is Carol's wedding ring, and an envelope sits next to the laptop. Mike sees the screen and her ring and immediately goes into the bedroom.

Once there, he doesn't see any of Carol's clothes on the bed. He goes into the closet to find all her clothes gone. He then looks in the drawers in the dresser and sees all her clothes are gone from there, too. When he goes into the bathroom and notices her sink and vanity area are completely empty, he realizes she's taken her things and left.

Mike comes back out to the living room, takes the letter out of the envelope, and reads it:

Mike, I've discovered the reason why you've been coming home late so many evenings. We've been together for over 5 years now and married for the last 3 years. I've never felt so betrayed by another person in my life. While I could have possibly understood a single picture where you were maybe out with friends or co-workers, what I found on your "Mighty Place" profile, which I didn't even know existed, was a full relationship with another woman. Multiple pictures taken on multiple occasions showing much more than just a friendship with a woman I've never seen or heard of. We're done. You'll receive divorce papers very soon. I no longer love you and no longer want you in my life. I've taken my things, and by the time you read this letter, I'll already be in another state. Please don't attempt to try and find me to explain yourself or your actions, because I don't care to hear your lies. I'll never allow you to hurt me again as you have. Goodbye, Michael.

Mike crumples the letter and throws it down, swearing as he does so, saying "Goddamn fuckin' bitch."

He sits on the couch, staring off into space, as if in deep thought. He looks over to the end table next to the couch and sees a utility bill with a "Disconnection Notice" stamped on the envelope. Under the envelope is a newspaper with a front-page title of "Phillip and Mary

Bates help over 200 animals find new homes". Under the heading is a picture of Phillip and Mary, and Mary has what appears to be a very expensive necklace around her neck. Mike just stares at the image.

* * *

The next day at the police station, Mike is sitting at a table, talking to Brian about Carol leaving him.

He says, "Her letter said for me not to look for her, because she'd be in another state by the time I read the letter."

Brian says, "Man, I'm sorry to hear that, dude. You're just getting shit flying at you from all directions, huh?"

Mike says, "Yeah, tell me about it. She even took the dog we just adopted. I called the shelter, and they said they'd called her to tell her the dog was ready and she'd already come in and picked it up. She took everything she owned out of that house. I'm alone now, man. I've got nobody left now. What am I supposed to do without Carol?"

Brian says, "I don't know, Mike, but I'm here for you if you need to talk. Anything I can do to help, you just let me know, okay?"

Mike says, "Yeah. I appreciate it, man. Thanks."

He and Brian then leave the break room.

CHAPTER 17

MARY BATES

Mike is in the 911 emergency response radio room, where calls come in and operators talk to police on the radio. On his computer, he's looking up the profile for Mary Bates, with a look of anger in his deep set evil eyes. The profile shows a Lexus registered to her, with a license plate MBates1; he recognizes that plate from the animal adoption agency parking lot. He then sees the address 101 Bellalago Drive.

A call comes in of a burglary in progress.

"911, what is your emergency?" the operator says, then pauses. "OK, what's the location?" The operator types the address into her computer. "OK, stand by. All units, 211 in progress. Bills Market, 1916 North John Young Parkway. Manager calling in says the suspect is being held at gunpoint."

As Mike listens to the radio operator make the call, he can hear the responding officer, Brian, call in over the radio.

"Unit 32 to base. Responding to 211 at 1916 North John Young Parkway."

The operator says, "Unit 32 responding to 211, copy."

Upset that he can't be there with Brian responding, Mike gets up from the desk and leaves the radio room.

* * *

Later that night, Mary Bates is driving down the road in her Lexus. A patrol car suddenly pulls up behind her, and the lights turn on to pull her over. She sees this and immediately gets on her cell phone to call Phillip, but the call goes to his voicemail. She pulls over to the side of the road and stops as she leaves him a message.

"Phillip, it's Mary. I'm being pulled over by the police. I'm on Gee Street, off Johnson." She sees Murphy getting out of his car. "Oh, God. It's that Murphy guy from the animal shelter. Call me as soon as you get this," she says.

Mary puts the cell phone in the door pocket down by her side just as Mike walks up to her side of the car and knocks on the window. As she lowers the window, he notices the very expensive necklace around her neck.

* * *

Phillip is in a meeting with clients regarding a real estate project when his assistant, Robert, comes in with an urgent phone call for him.

Phillip says, "And so, gentlemen, I think you'll understand the value to the city in approving my proposal for the development of this project."

Robert says, "Sir? You have a phone call."

Phillip responds, "Robert, I'm finishing up a meeting here. Please take a message for me."

Robert firmly says, "Sir, you need to take this call right now."

Phillip sees a look on Robert's face he's never seen before and realizes he must take the call. He tells his clients, "Uhh…excuse me just a moment, gentlemen." He then leaves the room with Robert.

* * *

Several police cars are now at the scene. A limousine pulls up with Phillip in the back and stops. He gets out and heads towards Mary's car, but 2 police officers stop him, sending him into a panic.

Captain Williams is up near Mary's car when he sees Phillip. He goes over to him, grabs him, and tells him he doesn't want to go to the car.

Williams says, "Phil, you don't wanna go up there. You don't need to see this."

Phillip says, "Jon, I need to see my wife."

Williams relents and tells the officers to let Phillip through. As Phillip slowly walks up to the car, Williams walks beside him. When they arrive at the vehicle, Phillip sees Mary dead in the front seat, slumped over behind the wheel. The necklace that was around her neck is missing.

Phillip breaks down and starts crying.

Phillip sits in his chair in his living room, crying while looking at a picture of Mary. His cell phone is on the end table next to his chair. The phone rings, and he answers it.

"Hello? Yes, Jon. I understand. Please let me know the results. Yes. Thank you. Goodbye."

Phillip hangs up the cell phone, then notices the icon in the top left corner indicating a missed call and voicemail. He swipes down the notifications to see a missed call from Mary about 2 hours earlier. He hits the notification for voicemail to listen to her message, his face suddenly erupting in anger and rage as he hears it. Once it's finished playing, he loudly calls for Robert, who quickly enters the room.

"Yes, Phillip, what is it?"

Phillip says, "Robert, sit down. We have a problem."

Robert sits down in Mary's chair next to him. Phillip continues.

"Robert, I need you to do something for me."

Robert says, "Yes, sir. Anything. What do you need?"

Phillip explains how he wants Robert to find the location of Mike Murphy. Robert leaves, then drives all evening before finally finding Mike at Al's Diner.

CHAPTER 18

PHILLIP BATES ARRAIGNMENT

Phillip is in the courtroom with Paul, to be arraigned for the murder of Officer Mike Murphy. The people are represented by District Attorney Brad James, a middle-aged, balding man, fairly slender, of average height and weight. Superior Court Judge Raymond Watkins, from the council meeting, is presiding over the case. The courtroom is filled with several people, including several African Americans present in support of Phillip Bates. The police chief, mayor, and Robert are also in the courtroom, standing in the back.

Judge Watkins starts the proceedings. "In the case of the State versus Phillip Bates, case #CR-55463, Mr. Phillip Bates, I am holding a copy of an indictment that has been handed down by the grand jury for the State of Arkansas, County of Jasper, charging you with one count of violation of code 187, capital murder in the first degree for the death of Michael Murphy, a human being, against the peace and dignity of the State of Arkansas. There are special circumstances related to this charge, as the victim was a police officer. Have you retained counsel, and do you wish to enter a plea at this time?"

Phillip stands. "I plead not guilty, Your Honor."

Goodwin then stands. "Your Honor, my name is Paul Goodwin. I am an attorney, and I represent Mr. Phillip Bates. We'd like to enter a plea of not guilty by reason of insanity."

The judge looks over to the court recorder, telling her to enter a plea of not guilty, then says, "The defense enters a plea of not guilty. Your trial is set for September first. All pre-trial motions and matters must be filed prior to this."

James, says, "Your Honor, due to the defendant's vast wealth and resources and ability to flee the country, as well as the extreme and horrific nature of the crime, and the fact that the victim was a police officer, we are requesting the defendant be held without bail at this time."

Goodwin responds, "Your Honor, my client has never been in trouble with the law. He could have very easily left the country immediately and disappeared forever following the alleged crime but instead turned himself in voluntarily. Also, the defendant is a highly-respected businessman, with over a dozen businesses in this city and numerous projects under development. He has a long history of helping people and helping this community. He does not like to see innocent people hurt or out of work. While the majority of his businesses will be able to remain open and operating as normal, some of the projects simply will not be able to continue at this time with him incarcerated. Furthermore, as you are already aware, he is a highly respected member of the city council and plays an important role in shaping the policies of this city."

The judge responds, "I am ordering bail for the defendant in the amount of ten million dollars, with a cash-only bond stipulation. I will also require that in the event bail is posted, the defendant will be required to wear an ankle monitor."

Goodwin says, "Your Honor, we would like to post bail."

The judge says, "I assumed as much. Very well. The defendant is ordered to surrender his passport. He is further ordered not to leave this state without prior permission of the Court. He is also ordered not to be in possession of any firearms or to commit any further violations that result in criminal charges. Any violation of these orders will result in the immediate forfeiture of bail and incarceration until trial." He looks at Phillip. "Do you understand, Mr. Bates? Are the instructions I just gave to you clear?"

Phillip responds, "Yes, Your Honor. I understand."

Looking at both attorneys, the judge says, "Anything else?"

Goodwin says, "Yes. Your Honor, rather than dragging this case out, my client would like to exercise his right to a speedy and public trial as soon as possible."

James opens his eyes wide in surprise, wondering why Phillip wouldn't want to take his time and push the trial out as far as possible to enjoy his freedom.

The judge says, "Very well. You are ordered to return in 45 days, on July first, for the start of trial. Jury selection will begin on that day."

Both attorneys thank the judge, who then says, "This court is now in recess for lunch until 2 PM."

Phillip is clearly pleased. As Phillip stands up, Goodwin tells him, "Well, that went better than I expected. I'll get the bail posted immediately and have you out in an hour or so, okay?"

Phillip says, "Thank you, Paul. You did good work here today. I'll see you soon."

James and Goodwin leave the courtroom, while the bailiff takes Phillip through the back.

CHAPTER 19

PAWN SHOP WITNESS

The next morning on Gee Street, near Johnson Avenue, a black sedan pulls up. Robert and Phillip, having been released on bail, exit the car. They're looking at the last place Mary was alive. Located across the street is the King Pawn Shop, a small pawn shop in town that's been open for several years. While Phillip and Robert are looking around the area where Mary was parked, a man comes out of the shop and runs up to both of them. He's a white man, approximately 30 years of age.

"Hello, my name is Paul. Mr. Bates, I just wanted to tell you I recognized you on the news, and I'm really sorry to hear about your wife."

Phillip thanks him and tells him he's very kind. Paul continues.

"I work at the pawn shop over there across the street. I saw the reports about what happened here with your wife, and with you and that cop in the diner. Our store was closed that night, but we have a security camera inside the store that points out the front door in case anyone tries to break in. Well, the camera caught all the activity going on over here that night. I watched the video, and it also caught what happened before all the cops showed up. Sir, a police car had your wife pulled over here for a couple of minutes before a bunch of cops showed up. It was dark and hard to see in the video, but you can clearly see a cop car with lights on and see an officer run back to the car and get in and take off. Then, about 5 minutes later, another cop shows up, and a cop gets out and walks up to the driver side window, and then about 2 to 3 minutes after that, a bunch of cops show up. I have the whole thing on video."

Robert and Paul look at each other, with very surprised looks on their faces. Robert then asks Paul, "Has anyone else seen this video or come into your store over there, asking any questions?"

Paul responds, "No. Like I said, we were closed that night. Nobody else has seen the video yet, since I'm the person who opened the store yesterday and today."

Robert says to Phillip, "Sir, I suggest you call your attorney right now and tell him about this."

Phillip agrees and places a call to Goodwin, while Robert continues talking to Paul. "Great work, kid. Think we can get a copy of that video?"

Paul says, "Sure. I'm a big fan of Mr. Bates. He helped my sister out a while back when she got into an accident and needed help. I'll do anything I can to help you guys."

About 10 minutes later, Goodwin arrives and gets out of his car. He approaches the three of them, and they continue to discuss what's happened. Goodwin asks Paul why he hadn't called the police to tell them about the video.

Paul says, "Well, after I saw the news report about Phillip's wife being murdered and then Phillip being arrested the next day for killing a police officer, I figured both incidents might be related. I knew Phillip was a good man because of all the stories I've seen about him, and because of what he did for my sister. I was hoping my video might be able to help him, and not hurt him. I wanted to try and help make that happen. And also, nobody ever came and asked me about it either, or I would have given it to them."

The four men walk across the street and into the pawn shop, where Paul gives his video disc to Goodwin and agrees to testify for Phillip if they need him to.

CHAPTER 20

START OF TRIAL

Reporter Melissa Childs is on camera, reporting on the start of the trial.

"Today, in the courthouse behind me, is the start of the historic trial of Phillip Bates, a man who is legendary in this community for his generous support of the people and the city. Mr. Bates is on trial for the murder of police officer Michael Murphy. While the state has declined to seek the death penalty for Mr. Bates, he is facing life in prison if convicted. The jury selection process took place yesterday. We'll keep you updated with information from the court as we get it. Reporting for WESH News, this is Melissa Childs."

The courtroom is packed. As Judge Watkins enters through his chamber door, the bailiff says, "All rise. This court is now in session. The Honorable Judge Raymond Watkins presiding."

Everyone rises as the judge walks up to his chair and sits down, then says, "Thank you, ladies and gentlemen. Please be seated. In the case of the People versus Phillip Bates, case #CR-55463, the jury selection of 12 jurors and 6 alternate jurors is complete. The primary jurors are now seated." He looks to D.A. James and says, "Counselor, you may begin with your opening statement."

James gets up and walks around his table to stand in front of the jury, looks at them, and begins speaking.

"Ladies and gentlemen, good morning. I want to begin by apologizing to all of you. I apologize for the fact that I'm going to have to take away several days of your life you'll never get back. I'm sorry I'll have to show you images and video that'll haunt you for the rest of your lives. Gruesome images like this…" He lifts a piece of white paper covering a board, with pictures of Officer Murphy dead on the floor. "And most of all, I'm sorry I have to be the one to prove to you beyond any reasonable doubt that those images are the result of the actions of the defendant, Phillip Bates, a man many of you may be familiar with. A man who's given a lot of money and help and support to the people in this city. A man now responsible for the gross execution of a police officer – A POLICE OFFICER – whose job it is to protect and serve you.

"Now, the defendant says he's not guilty of killing this officer. The defense is going to try to claim he was insane and didn't know what he was doing. Well, we'll be showing you security video footage of him walking into Al's Diner and executing that police officer. You'll hear from witnesses in that restaurant who watched him do it. You'll hear an expert in psychology who interviewed Mr. Bates explain how he knew exactly what he was doing. We'll show you beyond any reasonable doubt that the defendant, Mr. Phillip Bates, took the law into his own hands and murdered this police officer in cold blood and knew exactly what he was doing, and it'll be your job to decide what to do about it. Thank you."

James wasn't showing any emotion of any kind during his opening statement. His actions seemed to indicate that he was just trying to do his job and had no personal feelings either way about the defendant's actions.

As James returns to his seat and sits down, Watkins looks at Goodwin and says, "Mr. Goodwin, your turn."

Goodwin gets up and walks around his table to stand in front of the jury, then looks at them and begins speaking. From his tone, he appears angry at the opening statement of the prosecution.

"Ladies and gentlemen, good morning. I would also like to start by apologizing to you. I'm sorry that what you've just heard is an absolute lie. This trial is just now beginning, and we already have a lie coming from the D.A. He just told you Mr. Bates said he's not guilty of killing this officer. That is an absolute lie. Mr. Bates has never said he didn't kill Officer Murphy. The defendant has plead not guilty to MURDERING the officer. The prosecution just told you that you we'll be trying to claim the defendant is insane and didn't know what he was doing. That is also a lie. The defendant knew exactly what he was doing when he went into that diner and killed that officer. You see, in this great country, we have a concept called 'Irresistible Impulse.' Mr. Bates may have killed this officer, but he couldn't help himself or control his actions when he did it. A person suffering this condition is determined when a person knows what he's doing is wrong but is unable to control his or her actions. We'll be proving to you, beyond any reasonable doubt, not only that the defendant was unable to control his actions, but also why he took the actions he took. We'll be asking you to put yourself in the same situation the defendant was in and decide if you would have been able to control your actions under the same circumstances. You'll hear from a competent medical professional psychiatrist about the condition the defendant was suffering from, which prevented him from being able to control his own actions. Once you hear exactly what was going on in the mind of the defendant, and why he took the actions he took, it will be your job to determine whether or not he is was unable to control his actions. It will be your job to put yourself in the same place as the defendant and decide whether you would have been able to control your actions or not. And most important, it will be your job to determine whether the defendant is guilty and deserves to be punished. One thing I would like you to keep in mind in the coming days throughout this trial. Just because a person is charged with a crime, doesn't mean they have to be convicted of that crime. The defendant is not guilty until each and every one of you agrees that he is guilty and deserves to spend the rest of his life in jail. Thank you." He returns to his seat and sits down.

Watkins tells James, "The prosecution may call its first witness."

James stands up and says, "The People call Amy Silvers to the stand."

Amy Silvers comes through the door at the back of the courtroom, heads up to the witness stand, then stops before taking a seat to be sworn in.

The clerk says, "Please place your left hand on the bible and repeat after me." Amy does as instructed. "Do you solemnly swear the testimony you're about to give will be the truth, the whole truth, and nothing but the truth, so help you God?"

Amy responds, "I do."

The judge tells her to be seated, then James walks up and starts questioning her.

"Hello, Amy. Could you please state your full name and occupation for the record?"

Amy responds, "My name is Amy Silvers. I'm a student at DeVry University."

James says, "Very well. Now Amy, you were present in the restaurant at the time Officer Murphy was shot and killed. Can you tell us where you were seated here, using this diagram of the restaurant?"

He lifts the page, showing the photos of the dead officer on the board, pointing to a diagram of the cafeteria layout, with each booth numbered.

Amy says, "I was in booth number 10."

James responds, "Booth 10. And were you sitting on this side, or this side?"

Amy points and says, "That side," indicating she was on the side where she was looking directly at the booth with Officer Murphy's back to her. She would have been looking at Phillip's face while he was shooting Murphy.

James points and says, "This side? So, you were looking directly at the man who walked in and did this?"

Amy nods and says, "Yes."

James asks, "Now, is the man you saw come in and shoot the officer in this courtroom right now?"

Amy nods again and says, "Yes, he is."

James responds, "Could you please point to him to identify him?"

Amy raises her hand and points to Phillip Bates.

James says to the judge, "Let the record reflect that the witness has identified the defendant, Phillip Bates, as the man who walked in and killed the officer. Now Amy, can you tell us, did the defendant say anything to the officer prior to shooting him?"

Amy responds, "No, he just walked in, walked up to the officer, pulled out the gun, and started shooting."

James asks, "And how many times did he shoot the gun?"

Amy says, "I don't know. I wasn't counting. I was too scared. But he kept shooting until he didn't have any more bullets left."

James asks, "And how do you know he was out of bullets?"

Amy says, "Because the gun was one of those guns where you put the bullets in the handle. When he was out of bullets, the top of the gun was locked back."

James lifts the diagram of the layout of the diner, and the next page shows a revolver and automatic handgun.

James says, "Amy, these are 2 different types of handguns. Can you tell us which type of gun the defendant had?"

Amy says, "It was that one on the right."

James says, "Let the record reflect that the witness has identified an automatic handgun as the gun used to murder Officer Murphy." He grabs a paper from his desk. "Your Honor, I'd like to admit this into evidence," he says to Judge Watkins. "This is the coroner's report of the victim, Michael Murphy. The report indicates that the officer had a total of fifteen bullets in his chest and head. Now, the handgun identified by the witness is an automatic handgun that holds fifteen bullets. The witness has stated that the defendant kept firing until the gun was empty." He looks at the jury. "So, the defendant went in with a fully loaded automatic handgun and emptied the entire magazine into the victim." He looks back at the judge. "I have no more questions at this time, Your Honor."

Judge Watkins says to Goodwin, "Counselor."

Goodwin gets up from his desk and walks up to Amy.

"Hello, Amy. Now, you just identified the defendant as the man who came in and did this. Are you familiar with the defendant, or have you ever seen him before?"

Amy says, "Yes, I've seen him on TV several times."

Goodwin asks, "Several times? And the times you've seen him on TV, have they been because of this trial?"

Amy says, "Sometimes, but mostly because of him helping people." Goodwin says, "Helping people? I see. Do you think the defendant was a threat to anyone else in that restaurant or meant to hurt anyone else there?"

James says, "Objection, speculation. The witness surely isn't being asked whether or not a man standing in front of her shooting a police officer in the head multiple times is a threat to other people, is she?"

The judge says, "Sustained."

Goodwin continues. "I'll rephrase. Amy, did the defendant threaten anyone else in that diner by pointing his gun at anyone else or saying anything to anyone else?"

Amy says, "No, he didn't."

Goodwin asks, "OK. Now Amy, can you tell us what happened after the officer was shot?"

Amy says, "He turned and walked toward the front door, and right when he got there, he turned around and looked at the officer on the floor and said, 'You will never hurt another person again.'"

Goodwin says, "'You will never hurt another person again'? OK, what happened next?"

Amy says, "He turned and walked out the door and left. Then the police showed up."

Goodwin says, "OK, Amy, I have one final question for you. Did you personally feel you were ever in any danger from this man?"

Amy pauses for a moment, then looks at Phillip and says, "At first, when he first started shooting, I did. But then once he kept shooting at the same person and nobody else, I felt he wasn't there to hurt anyone else."

Phillip smiles at Amy. She sees him smile at her but doesn't show any emotion back as the whole courtroom is watching her.

Goodwin says, "Thank you, Amy." He then looks at Judge Watkins and says, "I have no further questions."

The judge tells Amy she may step down, then instructs the D.A. to call his next witness.

James says, "The People call Judy Baker."

CHAPTER 21

JUDY BAKER

Judy, the waitress from the diner, walks in from the back of the courtroom, approaches the witness stand, and takes the stand. She's then sworn in, and the D.A. approaches to question her.

"Hello, Judy. Can you please state your full name and occupation for the Court?"

Judy says, "Judy Lynn Baker. I'm a hostess and waitress at Al's Diner, on Fifth Street."

James asks, "Judy, can you please tell us what happened on the morning of March sixteenth of this year in the restaurant?"

Judy responds, "Yes. I was working the morning shift at the restaurant. I had several tables I was waiting on. One of my customers was a regular customer, police officer Mike Murphy. At one point, a customer came in and sat down in a booth up against the window. I gave him a menu and poured a cup of coffee for him, and I was facing toward the parking lot. I glanced up and happened to notice a man hugging another man. It seemed strange at first, but one of the men got into a car and drove off, so I figured maybe it was a brother hugging his brother, or maybe a dad hugging his son or something like that. After I saw that, I just went on with my work. I went to pick up an order that was ready to serve for one of my tables. I had a few plates in my hand, and I took them to the table at the end of the restaurant and set the plates down on the table. I still had a couple more to pick up for this table. Well, after I set down the plates, I turned to go towards the other end of the counter. Right when I took the first step, the other man who was hugging the first man had already entered the restaurant and was right in front of me, pointing a gun at the police officer. And he just started shooting over and over again, and I could see the blood splattering all over as he was hitting the officer in the head several times. I backed up and crouched down on the floor next to the booth I'd just served and screamed. The man looked like he ran out of bullets, so he turned around and started to walk toward the front door. When he got to the door, he turned around and looked at the dead officer on the floor and said the man would never hurt anyone else again. Then he walked out and got in a black car and drove off. Then a bunch of police showed up."

James asks, "Judy, was the man who did the shooting in this courtroom right now?"

Judy points to Phillip and says, "Yes, that's him there, Phillip Bates."

James looks to the judge and says, "Your Honor, let the record reflect that the witness has identified the defendant, Phillip Bates, as the shooter." He turns back to Judy. "Now Judy, had you ever met Mr. Bates prior to this event?"

Judy says, "Yes, I've met him once before."

James asks where and when they'd met.

Judy says, "I met him a few months ago, right before Christmas. I was in line at a Walmart, picking up a layaway, and he came in and paid off everyone's layaways, including mine. He also gave out gift cards to everyone in the store. I shook his hand and thanked him for that."

James says, "I see. So, you already knew who he was prior to this shooting, and you're certain it was him?"

Judy says, "Yes, it was definitely him."

James responds, "Thank you, Judy." He then turns to the judge. "Your Honor, at this time I'd like to play the security footage from the video system inside the cafeteria, showing what Judy and the last witness, Amy Silvers, have described in their testimony."

The judge asks Goodwin, "Does the defense have any objection at this time to the security video footage being played for the jury?"

Goodwin says, "No objection at this time, Your Honor."

The judge tells James he may proceed with the footage. James then goes over, turns on the TV, and starts playing the video. As the members of the courtroom and jury watch the footage, they react with shock at seeing the actual video of the shooting. Even Judy has a look of surprise as she watches it. Once the video ends, James turns off the TV and goes over to Judy to resume questioning her.

He says, "Judy, can you confirm that this is the video of the diner and the shooting incident?"

Judy responds, "Yes, it is."

James says, "Thank you, Judy." He turns to the judge. "I have no further questions at this time."

The judge tells Goodwin he may now proceed with his questioning.

Goodwin gets up, approaches Judy, and says, "Judy, I want to apologize first of all for you having to see that video. I'm sure that couldn't have been very pleasant for you, having to see that again. From watching the video, it's clear the defendant never once pointed the gun at anyone else or threatened anyone else. It appears he didn't even look at you during the entire time he was in the restaurant. Do you feel you were personally in any danger from this man, or do you feel he was only after this officer and meant no harm to anyone else?"

Judy says, "I think he was just after the officer. I was scared, but I didn't feel he would hurt me, especially once his gun ran out of bullets."

Goodwin says, "Thank you, Judy." He looks at Judge Watkins and says, "I have no further questions at this time, Your Honor."

The judge says to Judy, "You may step down now, Miss." He then speaks in general. "I think now would be a good time to break for lunch. We will reconvene here at 2 PM."

The courtroom clears out as people leave for lunch.

* * *

While at lunch, Goodwin talks to Phillip about the case.

"Phillip, the D.A. is going to be calling Murphy's partner, Brian Davis, after lunch. And I got word from another officer that their captain, a guy named Jon Williams, had to warn him and Murphy on several occasions about their conduct, and finally even suspended Murphy just before you killed him. They were both apparently on patrol together when Murphy shot and killed that Bubba Wilson kid who was all over the news a couple of months back. Well, his captain and Police Chief Dan Brady will both be in the courtroom today during Brian's testimony, so he isn't going to want to be lying when his job is on the line here. I'm going to really hammer him on the stand about these issues with Murphy's conduct and what kind of guy he was."

Phillip responds, "I know Jon and Dan personally. They're both very good friends of mine, and good people. They fly straight as an arrow. I told you before about how I had to warn Dan and ask him to personally watch these two officers after becoming aware of numerous incidents. These cops were really racist. Murphy had a history of insensitive behavior and actions towards minorities."

Goodwin says, "Well, it's all about to come out in court. In fact, one of the witnesses I have testifying for us later is a guy by the name of Walter Meyers. He owns a little market near Murphy's house. Well, apparently, his store was robbed by some black guy a few months back and Murphy was actually in the store at the time of the robbery according to what this Walter guy told me. Well this guy, Murphy, really beat the hell out of this guy that came in to rob it so bad that the guy fell into a coma. Walter told me that Murphy beat the guy to hell after the guy was disarmed and then Murphy and Davis, who showed up later, both threatened Walter telling him not to tell anyone about it. And also, apparently, he had a video security system in the store that recorded the whole thing, but Davis and Murphy made him give them the video disc and tell him to say the machine was broken. They completely lied about the whole thing. I got a copy of the police report with statements from both Murphy and Davis. I'm going to hammer Davis on the stand about this robbery and try and catch him in a lie. I'm going to make it clear Davis and Murphy were both real assholes."

Phillip responds, "That much is certain. Just remember, I don't want it to come out yet about him killing Mary. I want to bring that out myself when I take the stand."

Goodwin responds, "Got it. Not a problem."

They both finish their lunches over the next fifteen minutes while chatting about the case before heading back to court.

CHAPTER 22

BRIAN DAVIS TESTIFIES

The next morning, the courtroom is filled, and both lawyers are in place. Judge Watkins walks in, sits down, and continues with the case, instructing James, "Counselor, you may call your next witness."

James says, "The People call Brian Davis."

Brian enters the courtroom from the back and proceeds to the witness stand, where he's sworn in. James then starts his questioning.

"Mr. Davis, would you please state your name and occupation for the Court?"

Brian says, "Brian Davis. I'm a police officer for the Metro Police Department."

James asks, "And how long have you been a police officer?"

Brian says, "I've been a police officer for about 3 years."

James continues. "And are you familiar with the defendant, Phillip Bates, and the victim, Mike Murphy?"

Brian says, "I've seen the defendant on several occasions throughout my career. Mike Murphy was my partner for the last three years."

James asks, "The defendant is on trial for murdering your former partner. Are you aware of any reason why he may have done this, or are you aware of any case where your former partner had ever maybe threatened the defendant?"

Brian says, "Absolutely not. My partner wasn't like that at all. In all the time I've known him, I've never seen him threaten anyone with violence, other than threatening to arrest an individual in the line of duty. He was a great man. I became great friends with him the moment I first met him, when he helped me out of a tough spot, and I was very glad to have him as a partner ever since then."

James asks, "How exactly did Mr. Murphy help you out when you first met?"

Brian says, "The day I met him, he saved a man's life and prevented a riot from breaking out in the jail where I was working."

As James asks Brian to describe what happened the first time they met, Goodwin stands up.

"I object. How is this relevant to the charges against my client?"

James says, "Your Honor, the defendant is accused of walking into a diner and murdering a police officer in cold blood. I need to be able to show the jury that this is not just a case about a man's life being taken. It's about a valuable, experienced, and great resource being taken away from this city, because the victim was a police officer. The defense is portraying this man as a monster. I want to be able to show the court what kind of man he was and how he helped others."

The judge says, "I'll allow it. Objection overruled."

James says to Brian, "Please continue, Mr. Davis. Please tell us what happened the first time you met the victim."

Brian goes into detail regarding how he and Mike met.

"Well, I'd just made it onto the police force, and for my first assignment, I was sent to work doing guard duty at the detention center. It was my first day there. An officer brought in a prisoner who'd just been arrested on a DUI charge, and I had to take the prisoner back to his cell."

CHAPTER 23

DETENTION CENTER INCIDENT

Three years ago

A police car pulls up in front of the jail intake and brings in a prisoner. He's a white male. He isn't falling down drunk, but he's had enough drinks to put him over the legal limit to drive.

Brian is at the counter in the front of the detention center, training and doing intake work. Another jail guard sits behind the counter.

Brian asks the officer bringing in the prisoner, "Hey, what do we have here?"

The officer responds, "Suspicion of DUI. Here's the arrest form."

The officer takes off the suspect's handcuffs. The suspect then lowers his head onto the desk in front of Brian, who tells him to stand up straight.

He then tells the officer, "OK, we'll take it from here and get him booked in. Thanks." He turns to the suspect. "Hey, I need you to stand up straight, please."

The suspect stands up quickly and assumes a military position, like he's standing at attention. He then raises his right hand, gives Brian a salute, and sarcastically says, "Yes, sir."

Brian asks, "Are you okay, dude?"

The suspect points his finger directly at Brian and says, "I'm perfect!"

Brian asks, "And have you been drinking?"

The suspect puts his thumb and index finger very close together, then puts his fingers up close to his eye, as if trying to see how much space is between them, and tells Brian, "A little bit…umm…that much exactly," while showing Brian his fingers.

Brian rolls his eyes and smiles. The arresting officer who brought in the suspect just shakes his head, then turns around to leave.

He says, "OK, good luck. I'm outta here. See ya later."

Brian says, "Yeah, see ya."

Brian and the other jail guard come around the counter, take the suspect by the arms, and sit him on a bench while they do intake paperwork.

* * *

Back in the courtroom, Brian continues telling the Court what happened and how he met Mike Murphy.

He says, "We got the suspect booked into the computer, then we gave him his sleeping pad and took him back to the cell block to show him to his cell. And that's when all hell broke loose."

* * *

Brian and the other guard escort the prisoner down the corridor, bring him to the door at the end of the barracks, and open the door. As soon as they do, the prisoner starts freaking out.

He says, "Hey, wait a minute! I don't wanna be in there with them. I want my own cell. I don't wanna be in with other people!"

Brian says, "Yeah, well this isn't a five-star hotel. We can't all have everything we want now, huh? Your cell is right up there in the corner. Cell #24. The cell doors are on a timer. They'll open in a couple minutes. You can put your bedding in there when they open. You're on the top bunk."

The prisoner becomes very rude and angry, insulting Brian.

He says, "Hey Pig, I said I don't wanna fuckin' be in here. I wanna be in solitary. I don't wanna be in here with this shit."

Brian says, "No, what you really wanna do is just shut your mouth. Nobody cares what you want. Your cell is up there. Have a good night."

Brian closes the door and locks it. The prisoner kicks the door as Brian and the other guard walk off down the corridor, back towards the front.

The prisoner then yells out to them, screaming, "Let me outta here, man! I want my own fuckin' cell!"

Other prisoners start yelling at him, taunting and laughing at him, saying things like "Shut the fuck up, white boy," "Pussy," and "Yeah, come over here, you little bitch."

The prisoner looks around at the other prisoners in their cells, waiting for the timer to open so they can have their free time. He sees them all talking trash to him, laughing at him, making fun of him, and antagonizing him.

He throws his bedding down on the ground and yells, "Man, fuck this shit!"

He walks to the center of the barracks and climbs on top of a metal table in the middle, facing the other prisoners in their cells. He then yells at the other inmates locked in their cells in an angry, loud, commanding voice.

"OK, all you fuckin' niggers out there – listen up!"

All the other inmates stop yelling and laughing and just look at him, some with surprised and angry looks on their faces.

"What the fuck?" many of them say.

The prisoner continues. "In here, *I'm* the man! *I'm* in charge! You all do whatever the fuck I say, ya got it?" He looks around at the other inmates, then continues. "Who's the biggest, meanest motherfucker in here?"

As the prisoners in all the cells go crazy, yelling at and talking trash to the DUI inmate, Brian hears the commotion and head towards the cell block. The DUI inmate looks around, then zeros in on a very large Black inmate in a cell on the 1st floor in front of him.

He points his finger at the inmate and screams very loudly, "YOU, NIGGER! I OWN your Black ass! You do whatever the fuck I tell you to do, and if you don't like that arrangement, well, then FUCK YOU! FUCK YOU, you punk-ass bitch!"

The large prisoner is holding on to the cell door bars, shaking them violently, trying to open them, wanting to get out to come after the DUI inmate.

Suddenly, the timed cell door buzzers go off and the cells all unlock. The Black inmates all come charging out from multiple cells towards the DUI inmate. The large Black inmate he was screaming at is closest to him, and as he reaches the table and climbs up on it to smash the DUI inmate, the DUI inmate has a look of shock and fear on his face as he's violently jolted backward off the table onto the ground on his back.

Mike had suddenly rushed into the pod, yanked him off the table, and slammed him onto the ground. As he works to put handcuffs on him, Brian and the other officer move in front of him with their

Tasers drawn, aiming them down. Another jail guard comes rushing into the pod and draws his Taser as well.

Brian yells in a loud, commanding voice, "Stay back! Everyone, hold it right there. We'll handle this."

As the prisoners stop advancing towards the officers, the large Black inmate yells, "You better get that white boy's ass outta here quick!"

Mike yells at the DUI inmate, "You dumb son of a bitch! What the hell are you trying to do? Kill yourself?"

The inmate responds, "I told you I didn't want to be in here with these people. I want my own cell."

Mike says, "Yeah, well now you're gonna get exactly what you wanted. And you're gonna sit there and stare at the walls until your trial in about two months!"

The inmate yells back, "Good! Yeah, fuck all you niggers! *I'm* in charge!"

Mike yanks him up off the ground onto his feet and says,

"Alright, that's it. Let's go."

As he leads the inmate towards the door of the pod, the other prisoners shake their heads, some laughing. Some of them make comments like "Crazy white boy" and "Dumb punk ass." As Mike and the prisoner get near the door, the other guard opens it.

A Hispanic inmate near the door turns to look at the DUI inmate, who then looks at him and screams in his face, "What the FUCK are you lookin' at, BEANER?!!"

Mike forces the inmate out the door, and Brian follows behind him, holstering his Taser. The last guards then exit the pod, closing and locking the door on their way out. As Mike and the DUI inmate walk by the pod, the other inmates see them through the plexiglass.

The inmate taunts them, yelling, "I'm in charge! I'M IN CHARGE!"

Mike quickly slaps him on the back of his head and tells him to shut the hell up.

They finally arrive at the end of the corridor, where Mike locks the inmate in his solitary cell, then yells at him, "What the hell is wrong with you?! You don't pull that kind of shit in there. Those aren't people in there – they're fucking *animals* – and I just saved your life! Have a nice weekend!"

He slams the cell door shut and locks it, then turns around to introduce himself to Brian.

"Hey. How you doin'? I'm Mike Murphy."

He extends his hand to shake Brian's, who takes his hand, shakes it, and says, "Hey. Great to meet you, man. I'm Brian Davis. Thanks for helping me out in there, man. I thought that was going to be a riot in there."

Mike says, "Yeah, well, it would have been. You just have to show them who's boss in here. Be firm, but be fair with them. And don't take any shit from them either."

Brian says, "Yeah, I see that. Thanks. I'll remember that."

* * *

Back in the courtroom, Brian concludes his story about how he met Mike.

"And that's how I met him. He really helped me out of a jam that day, and we've been great friends ever since."

James asks, "So in your honest opinion, the victim, Mr. Murphy, was a good man?"

Brian says, "Absolutely. He was one of the best, honest, and fairest men I've ever known. And he was a good friend, and a good partner."

James says to the judge, "I have no further questions at this time, Your Honor."

Judge Watkins says to Goodwin, "Counselor, your witness."

Goodwin gets up, approaches Brian, and says, "Hello, Officer Davis. I just have a couple of questions here. You've said you've never seen Officer Murphy threaten anyone with violence, correct? Outside of threats to arrest someone, correct?"

Brian responds, "Correct. He's never threatened anyone with violence – except for threatening to place someone under arrest if that person didn't cooperate and do as they were told."

Goodwin then says, "Of course, we understand in the line of duty, while performing his job, he might have had to make threats like that to get a suspect to comply. But I'm referring to any incidents where he might have threatened a witness with violence. Have you ever seen him threaten or intimidate any witness with violence if the witness were to speak out on an incident?"

Brian says, "No. Never. I've never seen my partner threaten anyone like that."

Goodwin then asks, "OK, now do you recall an incident back on January fifth, when your partner was at a local market called 'Walt's Market,' where an armed robber came in to rob the store and your partner disarmed the robber and the robber ended up in a coma as the result of a severe beating by your partner?"

Brian says, "Yes, I'm familiar with that incident. The suspect resisted arrest and continued to go for his gun after my partner had disarmed him and told him he was under arrest. The suspect started fighting with my partner, and my partner had to exert additional force to apprehend him. Unfortunately, in the process, the suspect suffered trauma that resulted in him going into a coma."

Goodwin asks, "And after this suspect was beaten and arrested, did you or your partner in any way threaten the store owner, Walter, if he told anyone what he'd seen?"

Getting angry now, Brian firmly and loudly says, "Absolutely not. We never threatened anyone like that. That was a completely legal and justified arrest and action by my partner, and neither he nor I threatened anyone. And frankly, I resent the implication here that you're suggesting that either me or my partner would ever threaten or intimidate a witness."

Goodwin says, "Yeah, well, you'll just have to get over that. So, you're telling me and this jury that you didn't personally threaten the store owner, Walt, if he told anyone what he'd seen?"

Brian again says, "NO! Neither I nor my partner threatened him or anyone else."

Goodwin says, "I see. Now Officer Davis, this store had a camera security system. Did you tell the owner, Walt, to say the system was broken?"

James stands up and says, "Your Honor, I object. Clearly, the defense is attempting to smear and discredit the testimony of a police officer with a distinguished record of 3 years on the police force, which includes multiple citations and awards for his service."

The judge rules, "Overruled. Let's see where this takes us."

Brian, looking angry, says, "ABSOLUTELY NOT! No, I did *not* tell him to say that. In fact, both my partner and I asked the owner for the disc from the security system, and he told us the machine wasn't working."

Brian appears to have become increasingly agitated while on the stand, which was exactly how Goodwin wanted him to appear. As Brian was Murphy's partner, Goodwin was hoping to show the jury how easy a police officer can become upset under stress.

Goodwin says, "Thank you, Officer Davis." He turns to the judge. "I have no further questions for this witness."

Judge Watkins tells Brian he can step down, then tells everyone the Court will break for the day and reconvene in the morning.

CHAPTER 24

BARBARA JENSON

The next morning, with Court in session, Judge Watkins asks James, "Are you ready to call your next witness at this time?"

James says, "Yes, Your Honor. The People call Barbara Jenson."

Barbara comes in from the back of the courtroom, goes up to the stand, and is sworn in by the bailiff. James then starts questioning her.

"Hello. Could you please state your name and occupation for the record?"

Barbara says, "My name is Barbara Jenson. I'm an animal adoption specialist at the Humane Society."

James asks, "Are you familiar with the defendant, Phillip Bates?"

Barbara says, "Yes."

James asks, "How do you know him?"

She responds, "He and his wife, Mary, spent a day at our clinic before he was arrested. It was a special animal adoption event, where they were paying for all the adoption fees for the day for any customers who came in to adopt a pet."

James says, "Well, that's very nice. But the defendant is on trial for the murder of a police officer, Michael Murphy. Are you familiar with the victim?"

Barbara says, "Yes. He and his wife were customers who came in and adopted a dog that day."

James asks, "Can you tell us if you remember the defendant having any contact with the victim at that time, that you're aware of?"

Barbara says, "Yes. Phillip Bates and his wife personally met with each customer adopting a pet to thank them."

James says, "I see. And did you notice anything out of the ordinary when the defendant met the victim, Mr. Murphy?"

Barbara says, "Yes. Mr. Bates told the victim he could easily get him fired if he wanted to. And then after Mr. Murphy left, Mr. Bates's wife asked him what that was about. Mr. Bates said Mr. Murphy was a racist piece of crap and told his wife she should just stay away from him."

James asks, "You're saying the defendant called the victim a racist piece of crap and threatened to have him fired?"

Barbara says, "No. He didn't call him that directly. He told his own wife, Mary, that the officer was a piece of crap. And he only told the officer he could get an officer fired. He didn't say he was going to get him fired."

James then says, "I see. And what was the victim's reaction when Mr. Bates said this to him?"

Barbara says, "He just gave him a mean look and then told his wife Carol it was time to go. And then they both left."

James says, "And that's when the defendant called him a racist piece of crap?"

Barbara nods and says, "Yes."

James thanks her and tells the judge he has no further questions for her. The judge then tells Goodwin it's his turn, and Goodwin gets up and comes over to question her.

He says, "Hello, Barbara. Now, you stated the defendant said he could get an officer fired. What prompted that? I mean, it's unlikely he would have said that out of the blue for no reason. What did the officer say or do prior to this that would have prompted the defendant to say that?"

Barbara says, "Mr. Murphy threatened Mr. Bates."

Goodwin says, "Really? The victim, a police officer, threatened the defendant? Can you elaborate on that?"

Barbara says, "Well, Mr. Murphy told Mr. Bates he'd heard Mr. Bates had been talking to his boss, trying to get him in trouble. Mr. Murphy said he would always do whatever he had to do to protect his friends and family, and he told Mr. Bates he'd be wise to remember that."

Goodwin says, "The officer told the defendant he would do whatever he had to do to protect himself and he would be wise to remember that? And is that when the defendant told Mr. Murphy he could get an officer fired?"

Barbara nods and says, "Yes."

Goodwin says, "Thank you, Barbara." He turns to the judge. "No further questions."

The judge asks James if he'd like to redirect. James says yes, then comes up to Barbara to ask her one question.

"Barbara, can you tell us how close you were when this was going on? Could you clearly hear this conversation?"

Barbara says, "Yes, they were both right in front of me. I heard every word they both said. I didn't know Mr. Murphy was an officer at first, but I could tell they didn't like each other at all. I was surprised, because Mr. Bates has been there for several hours with his wife, and we had several friendly conversations with him, and I was surprised to hear what sounded like a threat from this officer. I expected to hear the officer and his wife thanking Mr. Bates for the adoption rather than making threats."

James says, "Thank you, Barbara. That's all I have."

Judge Watkins tells Barbara she can step down, then looks at his watch, which currently shows 11:00 AM. "Well, I think this would be a good point to break for lunch," he says. "The Court shall reconvene at two PM."

As the courtroom audience clears out, a Black woman named Rita Wilson, located a couple rows behind Phillip, stands up and waits for him as Goodwin turns to talk to him.

He says, "We need to have a quick talk to go over some strategy here."

Phillip says, "OK, sure. Over lunch?"

Goodwin agrees. As they both walk toward the back of the courtroom, Rita stops Phillip.

She says, "Excuse me, Mr. Phillip Bates?"

Phillip responds, "Yes?"

Rita walks up to him and extends her hand to shake hands with Phillip. Phillip shakes her hand and sees she has tears in her eyes. Phillip is surprised, as he doesn't know the woman.

She says, "My name is Rita Wilson, and that dirty bastard you killed murdered my son, Bubba. I just wanted to thank you for what you did. Bubba didn't deserve to die and certainly never pointed any gun at him. He killed my baby, and you killed him, and I'll be grateful to you for the rest of my life for that. And I also want you to know I'm prayin' for you here. I know the good Lord sees what a good man you are, and I feel you're gonna be okay here."

Phillip says, "Well, thank you very much, Rita. And I'm very sorry to hear about what happened to your son. I promised myself I'd never let that man hurt another person again after the things he did, and I meant it. I only wish I could have prevented the loss of your son."

Rita says, "Well, you've probably saved someone else's son, and God bless you for that, sir. I'll keep prayin' for you."

Phillip says, "Thank you. I appreciate the support. You have a great day, ma'am."

Phillip and Goodwin then leave the courtroom to go to lunch.

* * *

As they eat, Goodwin discusses the case with Phillip.

He says, "Well, the prosecution is just about done with their case. Showing the video hurt our case, but they don't know what we have planned yet. They have one more witness they're calling, and it's that doctor who interviewed you, Malcolm Harliss. He's going to try to convince the jury you weren't insane and knew exactly what you were doing and could have avoided doing what you did."

Phillip asks, "What's your plan to deal with him?"

Goodwin responds, "Listen, you're going to love this one. I hired a private investigator to dig up anything he could find on this Harliss guy. It took him quite a bit of digging. He even had to go back to people who knew this guy from his college days to find anything. He found solid gold. You want to know what he found for us that the prosecution doesn't even know about?"

Phillip says, "Tell me."

Goodwin says, "Here it is. Doctor Malcolm Harliss doesn't have a current license to practice medicine, because his license was revoked over two years ago. He's been illegally practicing either under a fake license or without a license at all, which is a felony in itself. The D.A. has no idea."

Phillip has a huge grin on his face as he asks, "Why was it suspended?"

Goodwin says, "Apparently, a former patient under his care was prescribed some medication by this doctor. Well, it turns out the doctor didn't first ask about the patient's allergies. I don't know all details, but apparently this patient suffered a seizure and died after taking what was considered an overdose because of his condition. Now, the doctor wasn't charged with any crime, because to avoid prosecution, he voluntarily agreed to the revocation of his license and

111

never to practice medicine again. He also lost a lawsuit brought by the family of the patient, and his insurance company had to pay a huge award. So, he's been practicing illegally now for over 2 years, with no license and no malpractice insurance. I'm going to absolutely destroy this guy on the stand. His testimony will be completely worthless to the prosecution."

Phillip asks, "This is going to make the D.A. look incompetent also, I would assume?"

Goodwin says, "Yes, to some degree. This doctor has testified at other trials over the past 2 years, so the D.A. probably didn't think there was any need to have a thorough investigation of him or his credentials done. Probably even figured he'd be saving some money on the trial also. Who knows."

Phillip says, "That is definitely excellent news to hear. I'm going to enjoy seeing this."

Goodwin says, "Yeah, I'm going to enjoy it, too."

CHAPTER 25

DOCTOR MALCOLM HARLISS

Back in court after lunch, Judge Watkins asks James, "Are you ready to call your next witness?"

James responds, "Yes, Your Honor. The People call Doctor Malcolm Harliss."

The doctor comes into the courtroom and is sworn in on the stand. He's a large, heavyset man, with a beard and mustache. He's professionally dressed in business attire. James starts his questioning.

"Please state your name and occupation for the Court," he says.

The doctor says, "My name is Doctor Malcolm Harliss. I'm a doctor of psychiatric medicine. I have my own practice, where I help individuals in need of professional psychiatric care."

James then asks, "Doctor Harliss, have you had a chance to examine the defendant, Phillip Bates?"

The doctor responds, "Yes. I spent several hours interviewing and researching him in preparation for this trial."

James asks, "And are you fully aware of the charges against the defendant and the circumstances of this case that resulted in these charges?"

Harliss responds, "Yes, I am."

James asks, "And after all your research and interviews with the defendant, can you give us the results of your research? The defendant is claiming he was insane and had no ability to stop himself from walking into a crowded cafeteria and pulling out a handgun and emptying the entire magazine into the head and chest of a police officer. What is your response to that? Do you feel he was insane and unable to avoid taking this action?"

Harliss says, "Absolutely not. In my professional opinion, the defendant was in full control of his actions and could have avoided this entire situation. He knew exactly what he was doing. It was very clear from my examination that he took the time to prepare for this action. After he killed the man, the police went to his house, looking for him. He wasn't there. A man at his house said he'd given him a card to give to the police for his attorney. The fact that he made such preparations to plan for the arrival of the police and had already planned on turning himself in indicates a level of planning not consistent with a person who's insane."

James says, "Thank you, Doctor." He turns to the judge. "I have no further questions at this time, Your Honor."

The judge tells Goodwin it's his turn. Goodwin gets up to come and start his questioning of the doctor, the paperwork provided by his private investigator in his hand.

Goodwin says, "Doctor Harliss, you said you have your own practice. Could you please tell us how many patients you're currently seeing?"

Harliss responds, "I currently have forty-seven patients I see on a regular basis."

Goodwin says, "Forty-seven. And these forty-seven patients you're seeing, I assume they're for various psychiatric needs?"

Harliss says, "Yes, correct. They have various needs. Some need more specialized care than others."

Goodwin asks, "And do some of these patients require prescriptions for medication also?"

Harliss says, "Yes. I provide prescriptions, when necessary."

Goodwin asks, "Doctor, can you tell the Court about your experience? How long have you been practicing medicine?"

Harliss says, "I've been practicing medicine for eight years."

Goodwin asks, "And what licenses do you currently hold?"

Harliss says, "I have an MD degree from Arkansas State University, and I hold a license from the Arkansas State medical board for practicing medicine."

Goodwin asks, "Doctor, how many trials have you testified in as an expert witness?"

Harliss responds, "This would be my thirty-eighth trial in eight years. I've testified as a witness for the defense and prosecution in numerous trials."

Harliss appears very confident in his testimony, as well as very relaxed and comfortable on the stand; he has no idea Goodwin is fully aware of his prior license suspension and illegal practice.

Goodwin says, "Now Doctor, I just have a couple of final questions here for you. Have you ever been convicted of a felony?"

Harliss responds, "Absolutely not. I've never been charged with or convicted of any crimes."

Goodwin asks, "Because you've never been caught yet?"

Harliss forcefully responds, "BECAUSE I HAVEN'T COMMITTED ANY CRIMES."

Goodwin asks, "Are you sure about that?"

James stands up, shouting, "Your Honor, I object. The defense is attempting to discredit a well-qualified doctor and smear his good name before this jury. His statement is an insult to the witness, and to this courtroom."

Goodwin says, "Your Honor, if I may be allowed to proceed, I have evidence here that not only directly disputes the testimony given by this witness, but also very clearly indicates the doctor here is currently committing a felony."

Harliss's eyes open wide, and he appears almost frozen, not showing any emotion other than surprise. James also has a surprised look on his face.

Judge Watkins, looking directly at Goodwin, says, "This better be good. Let's see where this takes us. Objection overruled."

Goodwin says, "Thank you, Your Honor. Doctor, you said you're currently running your own practice, with forty-seven patients. And you're currently licensed to practice medicine. Doctor, are you telling this Court your license wasn't revoked almost two years ago after one of your patients died following a drug overdose from drugs prescribed by you? You're telling this Court you aren't committing a felony by illegally practicing medicine without medical insurance and without a license for over two years? You're telling this Court your medical malpractice insurance wasn't forced to pay a multimillion-dollar settlement on your behalf as a result of your practice and your license was revoked as a result of this incident? I'll ask you one last time, Doctor. Do you currently hold a valid license to practice medicine?"

Harliss, looking almost dizzy, responds, "No, my license is not current."

James's hands cover his face, as he feels greatly embarrassed by the turn of events. Several loud gasps are heard from the people in the courtroom who are shocked.

Goodwin says, "Thank you, Doctor." He turns to Judge Watkins. "I have no further questions for this witness."

The judge has a very stern look on his face as he glares at Harliss and tells him he's excused.

Goodwin looks over to James and says, "I guess I just brought you boys some new business, huh?"

Phillip just stares at James, who's too embarrassed even to look at either Phillip or Goodwin.

Judge Watkins asks, "Are the People ready to call their next witness?"

James stands up and says, "Your Honor, at this time, while we reserve the right to call rebuttal witnesses, the State rests its case."

The judge says, "Very well. We'll break for the day. The defense will present its case tomorrow."

CHAPTER 26

WALTER MEYERS TESTIFIES

The next morning, Goodwin and Phillip are meeting at the courthouse to discuss a new development. Goodwin explains to Phillip how he'd been contacted the prior evening after court by Walter Meyers. Walter had been in court and watched Brian Davis testify about how he and Mike Murphy had never threatened anyone, and he was infuriated that Brian would tell such an absolute lie on the stand.

Goodwin says, "Well, Walt told me something last night that he hadn't told me before when I interviewed him. He told me when he gave the video disc from his security system to these cops, he made an additional copy of the video himself. I had him come down to my office last night with this video, and we both watched it. It clearly shows the police threatening him and disputes all the testimony given by Brian. I'm going to be calling Walter as our first witness this morning, and I'm going to try and introduce this video into evidence. Also, immediately after seeing the video, I left a message for Brian's captain, Jon Williams, letting him know he might want to be in court himself this morning to hear the testimony showing how one of his officers committed perjury on the stand."

Phillip says, "What do you mean you're going to try and get the video admitted? Can't you just request to play it?"

Goodwin responds, "Yes, but the D.A. is going to object to this because he won't have had any opportunity to review the video himself. I'll respond that I was just made aware of the video last night. He'll also try and object, saying the video hasn't been authenticated by a video or audio expert. I'll counter that the video doesn't need to be reviewed for authenticity because the person who made the video himself, Walter, is in court and on the stand right in front of us. The judge could rule the video inadmissible in this case, but I doubt he will, considering it directly refutes the testimony given by a sworn police officer. Especially if the police captain shows up in court, too. Also, during discovery, the D.A. legally has to turn over everything they have to us. And while it's customary for us to turn over what we have to them, we don't have to legally turn over every single piece of evidence we have. And I didn't even come into possession of or even knowledge of the existence of the video until last night."

Phillip says, "Well, that is excellent news, Paul. Great work. Let's hope for the best today."

Goodwin says, "Thank you. I think it'll go okay. Well, it's time. We better get to court."

Both of them leave the room and head into the courtroom.

* * *

With the courtroom now filled and the judge and jury in place, Judge Watkins calls on the defense to call its first witness.

Goodwin says, "The defense calls Walter Meyers."

James bolts to his feet. "Objection, Your Honor! How is this witness relevant to the charges against the defendant?"

Goodwin says, "Your Honor, this is a rebuttal witness called to refute testimony given by the previous witness for the prosecution. This goes to the heart of the credibility of the witness."

The judge says, "Overruled. I'll allow the witness. You may proceed, Counselor."

Walter comes in from the rear of the courthouse, takes the stand, and is sworn in by the bailiff. Goodwin stands up and approaches the witness to start his questioning.

He says, "Hello, Mr. Meyers. Can you please state your name and occupation for the record?" he asks.

Walt responds, "Walter Meyers. I'm the owner of Walt's Market, on 4th Street and Highland."

Goodwin asks, "Now Mr. Meyers, were you the victim of a robbery attempt at your market back on January fifth of this year?"

Walt responds, "Yes. A young man came in that day and attempted to rob me at gunpoint."

Goodwin continues. "OK. Can you please explain to us what happened in that incident?"

Walt says, "I was helping out a customer when this off-duty cop, Mike Murphy, comes in for some stuff. I knew him by name because he was a regular who would come in all the time. Anyway, he was in the back of the store when this young Black dude comes in and

118

points a gun at me and starts screaming at me to give him my money. Well, Mike heard what was going on from the back of the store, and before the dude could do anything, Mike ran up behind him and clocked him right in the face. The dude dropped his gun and fell to the floor and was barely conscious. I thought it was just awesome. But then Mike comes up and grabs the kid, and while he's holding on to the kid, he starts punching him over and over again. I thought he was going to kill him. And he was calling him a worthless nigger and a bunch of other stuff while he was punching him. I had to tell him to stop before he killed the dude."

Goodwin asks, "So, you're saying he kept punching the guy and making racial statements while punching him, after the suspect was already disarmed and posed no further threat to you?"

Walt says, "Yes. The guy was totally out of it. I don't think Mike needed to keep beating on the dude. It seemed like Mike had some kind of a personal vendetta against the dude or something, the way he kept beatin' on him."

Goodwin then asks, "And did Mr. Murphy stop his assault on the suspect when you told him to stop?"

Walt says, "Well, I yelled out to him twice, saying, 'Mike, that's enough.' He stopped after the second time I yelled to him."

Goodwin asks, "What happened next?"

Walt says, "Mike threatened me! He told me not to tell anyone about what had just happened, and he demanded the disc from my security camera system. And then his partner, Brian, came in and threatened me, too."

Goodwin says, "Mike threatened you and took the video surveillance disc? So, you're saying your security system worked and Officer Murphy demanded the video disc? And his partner threatened you, too? What kind of threat? What did they say?"

Walt says, "They threatened to come back and cause trouble for me and make my life 'complicated' if I told anyone what had happened. They wanted me to lie for them and tell them the dude had kept resisting, and that was why he was beaten so bad. And they wanted me to say the cameras weren't working."

James bolts to his feet again. "Objection! The defense is attempting to build its case on evidence that doesn't even exist. There was no security video disc in the arrest report, and the witness gave a sworn statement to the investigators after the robbery that the video system wasn't working."

Goodwin counters with, "Your Honor, the witness was in fear of his safety and made the statement to police because of that fear. He turned over the video disc to Murphy because he feared for his safety. However, what the D.A. and Mr. Murphy and his partner failed to realize was that the disc the witness gave to Mr. Murphy was just a copy of the recording in the machine. Walter here also made a second backup copy." He gets a disc off his desk and holds it up for the judge to see, then says, "Your Honor, here's a copy of the video security disc from Walt's store of that robbery. The entire incident is on video, which will prove the previous witness for the State, Police Officer Brian Davis, perjured himself on the witness stand by making several false statements, as well as tampering with a witness. I would like to play this video for the Court at this time. It will clearly show the previous witness for the State lying."

James says, "Your Honor, we're objecting to this video being played. We weren't given a copy of this video and weren't even aware of its existence. We have no way to verify the authenticity of the video or when it was created."

Goodwin says, "Your Honor, I have here a copy of the arrest report for that suspect who was beaten into a coma by Officer Murphy. The authenticity will be proven not only by viewing the video and looking at the picture of the robbery suspect in this arrest report, but also by the fact that the video itself was made by the security system belonging to the witness currently on the stand, who has sworn to tell the truth."

Judge Watkins says, "Because of the seriousness of the evidence and its potential to show perjury being committed by one of our own police officers, I'm overruling the objection. The evidence will be allowed." He looks at Goodwin. "You may proceed, Counselor."

Goodwin takes the DVD over to the TV, turns it on, then puts the disc in the DVD player to play it. The video of the robbery from the surveillance appears, and while it's playing, Police Chief Dan Brady, who's in the courtroom, looks surprised and angry as he watches his officers threaten Walter and demand the video disc.

As the video ends, Goodwin approaches the witness box and asks, "Walter, were you afraid of these officers at the time they were threatening you?"

Walt responds, "Yes, I was. I was more scared of them than I was of the dude who'd come in to rob me. I thought right then if I didn't do what they told me, they might beat me like they did that kid. I thought to myself there was no way these guys should be cops neither."

Goodwin then asks, "Can you tell us why you decided to come to me with this video this morning, rather than show it to the police department a long time ago?"

Walt replies, "I felt it was the right thing to do after seeing that officer testify the other day, calling me a liar. And I felt since the police had already taken my other copy of it and then lied about it, what's to stop them from doing it again? I've seen what this man on trial has done for people, how he's helped a lot of people, and I believe he's a good man. I didn't like seeing this Brian dude on the stand here the other day, lying about the whole thing. And I've seen how bad the man is who was killed. I wanted people to know what kind of man he was. And also, I knew he couldn't do anything to me anymore now, since he's dead."

Goodwin says, "Thank you, Walter." Turning to the judge, he says, "I have no further questions at this time."

The judge tells James it's his turn.

James rises, approaches Walter, and starts his questioning by asking, "Walter, this kid came in to rob your store and pointed a gun at you and demanded your money. Do you feel the actions of the murdered victim, Officer Mike Murphy, prevented that robbery from succeeding?"

Walt nods and says, "Yes."

James continues. "And were you in fear of your life when the suspect had that gun pointed at you, demanding your money?"

Walt again nods and replies, "Yes."

James then asks, "And were you in fear of your life immediately after Officer Murphy disarmed the suspect?"

Walter looks directly at the jury and says, "Yes, from the cops!"

People in the courtroom erupt in laughter, and Phillip and Goodwin smile before the judge yells out, demanding order in the courtroom.

James gives Phillip an angry look, then asks, "Were you in fear of the robbery suspect who'd been pointing a gun at you after Officer Murphy disarmed the suspect?"

Walter says, "No."

As James says he has no further questions and turns to head towards his desk, Walter looks directly at the jury and addresses them.

"That man," he points to Phillip, "is a good man. And those cops were bad dudes. They should never have been cops."

James turns back around with an angry look on his face and yells at the judge.

"Your Honor, I want that witness silenced!"

The judge orders the jury to disregard Walter's last comment and tells Walter he needs to step down, then orders a break for lunch. As Walter gets up and steps down from the stand, Phillip and Goodwin both smile at him.

CHAPTER 27

PHILLIP BATES TESTIFIES

Melissa Childs is outside the courthouse, reporting on the 3rd day of the case, as well as on the investigation into the gun that killed Bubba Wilson.

"Now into the third day of the murder trial of Phillip Bates, and the big question everyone is asking is, will Mr. Bates take the stand in his own defense? He's on trial for the murder of police officer Mike Murphy, who was under investigation in the shooting death of a handicapped teenager, Bubba Wilson, at the time he was killed. Officer Murphy claimed Bubba Wilson had pointed a handgun at him, something his family vehemently denies, as he'd never owned or fired a gun and was mentally incapable of doing so. And we've just learned an internal investigation by the police department has revealed that the gun found in Bubba's hand, which was allegedly pointed at Officer Murphy, in fact was recorded into evidence in the police department's own property room. What effect this might have on the trial of Phillip Bates is unclear. We'll provide more details as they come to us. Reporting from the courthouse, I'm Melissa Childs, for WESH News, mid-day."

Back inside the courtroom, Goodwin stands up and says, "Your Honor, I call to the stand the defendant, Phillip Bates."

Phillip gets up, approaches the bench to take the stand, and is sworn in to testify. Goodwin then approaches him.

"Mr. Bates. You've been charged with the murder of police officer Mike Murphy on March sixteenth, at Al's Diner. We've heard from several witnesses now. We've seen video of the event from surveillance cameras at the diner. Can you tell us, in your own words, what happened on the morning of March sixteenth?"

Phillip says, "Yes. I walked into that diner that morning, and I killed that officer."

The courtroom erupts in a lot of noise. The jury – and even the judge and D.A. – look shocked to hear him admit to the killing so easily.

Judge Watkins then says, "OK, everyone, let's have some order here."

Goodwin says, "Can you please elaborate for us?"

Phillip continues. "I drove down to the diner in the morning after becoming aware that the officer was eating breakfast there. I pulled into the parking lot, got out of my car, and walked into the diner. I walked up to the officer, about five feet away from him. I pulled out a .45 caliber automatic handgun and shot him. I emptied the entire clip into him to make absolutely sure he was dead. I didn't say anything to him or even give him a chance to fight back or apologize for what he'd done. I just killed him. I knew exactly what I was doing. I was not under the influence of any drugs. Nobody forced me, threatened me, or paid me to do it. I made the decision all by myself and took the action all by myself, and nothing was going to stop me. I had to do this."

Goodwin then asks, "Can you tell the Court why you took this action?"

Phillip responds, "Because that man was a murderer and completely racist piece of crap and I had to prevent him from killing again."

The courtroom erupts with noise at Phillips description of the police officer.

The judge says, "Alright, I said I want some order in this courtroom."

Goodwin says, "Please elaborate, Mr. Bates."

Phillip says, "I first became aware of Mr. Murphy after an incident in which he beat a Black suspect so severely, the man had to be transported to the hospital. This beating took place in the back of the police car driven by his partner, Officer Brian Davis. Mike Murphy was the passenger. The man who was beaten was already under arrest, in handcuffs, in the back seat of the car. A short time after this, officer Murphy was involved in another incident in which he beat a Black man so severely, the man ended up in a coma. This was the incident at Walt's Market shown in previous testimony. In both incidents, I'd given the police chief a warning to keep an eye on this officer and his partner. However, despite my warnings, the officer was then involved in the shooting of an unarmed, mentally handicapped Black teenage man after claiming the man had pointed a gun at him. Only then was the officer put on desk duty. This is the whole 'Bubba Wilson' investigation currently taking place."

Goodwin addresses the judge. "Your Honor, these are the three police reports obtained from the police department, citing the incidents just described by the defendant. And here's a copy of the report I was given this morning, indicating that the handgun Officer Mike Murphy says was pointed at him had actually been recorded into evidence in the police department's own property room, a room Officer Murphy was able to access." He then turns back to Phillip. "Mr. Bates, have you ever personally met this officer prior to the diner incident?"

Phillip says, "Yes. I met him at an animal adoption event, at which point he threatened me for talking to his police chief when I gave a warning to him to watch his men, as I spoke of earlier."

Goodwin asks, "How were you threatened?"

Phillip says, "He told me I should keep in mind he'll always do whatever he has to do to protect himself, his partner, his family. Stuff like that. I considered it a personal threat."

James says, "Objection, hearsay."

The judge says, "Sustained."

Goodwin continues, "Mr. Bates, can you tell us what happened the night before you killed this officer? The night of March fifteenth?"

Phillip replies, "Yes. The night before I killed this officer, my wife was pulled over by a police officer. That police officer robbed my wife of a very expensive necklace, then killed my wife by snapping her neck. That officer was Mike Murphy."

The courtroom erupts, and the judge, jury, and prosecutor all have shocked looks on their faces.

James stands up and says, "Your Honor, I object! The People are aware of the death of the defendant's wife the night before he murdered the officer. However, while the defendant has our sympathy for the death of his wife, there is no evidence to prove or even suggest that Officer Mike Murphy or any other officer was involved in the death of his wife."

Goodwin holds up a disc and addresses the judge. "Your Honor, this disc contains a voicemail from Mary Bates, the wife of the defendant, to her husband, Phillip Bates. The voicemail recording takes place during the entire incident, and here is a copy of the phone bill showing the call being placed from the defendant's wife. I would like to play this recording for the Court. You'll see the time stamp and length of the call matches the information shown on the bill."

The judge says, "Very well. Proceed. Objection overruled."

Goodwin plays the recording. As it airs, Phillip, on the stand, has tears coming from his eyes. After the recording ends, the judge, jury, and D.A. are very shocked to realize Mike had really murdered Phillip's wife.

James stands up and says, "Your Honor, I object. We have no way of knowing when the recording was made. It could have been made any time prior to this incident."

Goodwin responds, "Your Honor, I anticipated this objection, which is why I provided the matching phone bill. Now, I would like to present this evidence." Holding up a cell phone, he says, "This is the defendant's cell phone at the time of his arrest. This is the phone he was actively using for his daily business on the night before his arrest. The original voicemail is still in the voicemail box, and this phone is still active. We can make a call on speakerphone right here and now and listen to the voicemail recorded directly on Verizon phone servers. The voicemail has the time and date on it." Looking over at James, Goodwin says, "If the D.A. wishes to hear the same message again coming directly from Verizon servers, we will be happy to play the message again."

James realizes he has no winning objection and shakes his head, indicating he doesn't want to hear the message again.

The judge says, "Objection overruled."

Phillip says, "He threatened me. Then he killed that kid and placed his own stolen gun in that kid's hand. And then he murdered my wife. So, I killed him. It was only a matter of time before he would have killed another innocent person. I wasn't going to allow that. I had no choice here."

Goodwin says, "No further questions at this time, Your Honor."

The judge asks James if he would like to cross-examine the witness.

James rises and asks, "Mr. Bates. First, I want to say I am sorry for the loss of your wife. I'd like to ask why you didn't go to the police with this voicemail? Why you felt you had the right to take the law into your own hands instead of allowing the police to handle it?"

Phillip says, "That man had two separate incidents of beating minority individuals. Then he killed a handicapped black teenager before placing a stolen gun in his hand and blaming the kid for the incident. The police didn't handle those three incidents. And despite my warning to the police chief, the officer was still allowed to remain in a position to pull my wife over before killing her. That was the final straw. There was absolutely no way I was even going to take a chance on allowing that man to hurt or kill someone else. After he killed my wife, I went into a rage and I went and put a tunnel through his head. I don't regret what I've done, and I'd kill him again in a heartbeat under the same circumstances. It was time for him to die."

The courtroom erupts in applause, prompting the judge to exclaim, "That's enough! Another outburst like that in here, and you'll all be outta here. Continue, Mr. James."

James says, "Mr. Bates, you've admitted to this Court that you did indeed shoot and kill Officer Mike Murphy. Yet when you came down to the police station to surrender, you didn't have the firearm in your possession. My question is, where is this firearm?"

Phillip responds, "I was surrendering because I was wanted for questioning regarding the death of this officer. Once I was charged, I was ordered not to be in possession of any firearms. So, I had my associates remove all firearms prior to my arrival home after being released from custody."

James asks, "And where is that firearm now?"

Phillip says, "It has been destroyed."

James says, "You destroyed it? You destroyed the evidence you used to commit this crime?"

Goodwin rises and says, "Your Honor, I object. The D.A. is trying to badger and intimidate the defendant. The defendant was under no legal obligation or requirement to surrender this firearm, and the D.A. knows this. He's just trying to make the defendant look bad in front of the jury by implying the defendant was trying to deliberately hide evidence, even though he was fully within his right to have his personal property destroyed once he was ordered not to be in possession of them."

The judge responds, "Objection sustained."

James continues. "Mr. Bates, you have pleaded not guilty by reason of insanity, claiming you had no ability to control your actions here. Yet from the evidence, it appears you have gone through a great deal of preparation and planning before committing this crime and then already having a plan in place to surrender and defend yourself. It seems you could have changed your mind at any time and gone about this a different way. My question is, what exactly forced you to take these actions you claim you were completely unable to control?"

Phillip responds, "As I said before, once I realized he'd killed my wife, I went into a rage and felt I had no other choice. I felt he would kill again if he wasn't stopped immediately."

Because Phillip has known James for years, he's very familiar with his family – including his wife, whom he notices in the courtroom a few rows behind James.

Phillip continues. "Brad. I've known you for years. I know your wife and kids. I know your wife is here in the courtroom right now. You tell me, if Mike Murphy had killed your wife and two children, how would you respond?"

James looks at his wife, then looks back at Phillip for a moment. He then turns to the judge and says, "Your Honor, I have no more questions for this witness."

The judge tells Phillip he can step down from the witness stand, then announces the Court will break for the day.

* * *

The next morning, as Goodwin is heading towards the courthouse, he notices something different in town as he's driving. The roads have unusually light traffic, and many businesses, stores, and restaurants don't appear to be open. Paul looks down at his watch to see the date, wondering if maybe today is a holiday that he'd forgotten about; it's not.

As Goodwin comes to about a half-mile from the courthouse, he quickly realizes why: He's looking at what appears to be most of the residents of the city at the courthouse, in support of Phillip. There are so many people, the police are having to control traffic. The police wave Goodwin through so he can park and get inside. After he does, he goes into the courthouse and is taken into the back, where Phillip currently is talking with Robert. As Goodwin comes in, he asks Phillip and Robert if they're aware of the crowd outside. Phillip tells Goodwin how he and Robert were just talking about the crowd and how it appears much of the city is idle, as hundreds of people have taken the day off to come support him.

* * *

Later, with the Court back in session, the judge asks Goodwin if he's ready to call his next witness.

Goodwin responds, "Your Honor, the defense calls Mr. Paul Walker."

CHAPTER 28

PAUL WALKER TESTIFIES

Paul Walker walks into the courtroom and takes the witness stand after being sworn in.

Goodwin starts his questioning by asking, "Hello Paul, could you please state your full name and occupation for the record?"

Walker responds, "My name is Paul Walker. I'm the manager of the King Pawn Shop on Gee Street."

Goodwin asks, "And are you familiar with the defendant, Phillip Bates?"

Walker responds, "Yes, I met him after he was arrested."

Goodwin asks, "Okay, now Paul, can you tell us where you were on the night prior to the defendant's arrest? The night of March fifteenth?"

James stands up and says, "Your Honor, I object. What relevance does the night prior to this even have on the charges against the defendant?"

Goodwin responds. "Your Honor, the defendant has plead not guilty by reason of temporary insanity. The defendant has testified that he did, in fact, kill this officer. Our intention is to prove that the defendant was unable to control his actions. We certainly can't prove that without showing what happened the night before and leading into the morning of the crime. The defendant has stated this officer murdered his wife the night before the officer was shot. This witness has been called to help establish proof that the defendant's wife was, in fact, killed by this officer. Now, we would be happy to withdraw this witness if the State is willing to concede that the officer did murder the defendant's wife the night before he was killed by the defendant?"

James responds, "We aren't willing to concede anything."

The judge says, "Objection is overruled. The witness can testify."

Goodwin says, "Thank you, Your Honor." Looking at Walker, he continues. "Paul? Can you tell us where you were and what you saw on the night of March fifteenth?"

Walker says, "I was working at my pawn shop alone on Gee Street that night. Across the street, around nine PM, a car was pulled over by a police officer. I wasn't really paying much attention, since I had so much work to do. Anyway, I continued doing some work, and then when I looked back out, about ten or maybe fifteen minutes later, there were a whole bunch of cop cars there. I just figured someone was getting arrested or hurt or something maybe. But then the next day, it was all over the news what had happened about Mr. Bates and about his wife being killed. Well, I didn't connect the dots until Mr. Bates and his attorney showed up at that same spot across the street from my shop the next day. Well, while they were across the street, I went back and watched the video from the security camera and saw the person getting pulled over by the cop and the cop leaving a couple minutes later, and the car stayed there. And then another cop car came along and the officer got out of the car and came up to the car slowly, almost like he was investigating or something like that. Well, once he got up to the driver side window and shined a flashlight in the window, he ran back to his car and made some kind of call on his radio or something, and then that's when all the other cops started showing up pretty quickly. Well, I went across the street when I saw Mr. Bates and his attorney there and told them about what had happened the night before and what I had seen, and I gave them a copy of the video security disc."

Goodwin responds, "Thank you, Paul. Your Honor, here is the disc Paul here gave to us. I would like to show it to the Court so the Court can get an idea of what had to be going through the defendant's mind. As you'll see in the video, just before the video ends, the defendant is seen arriving and coming up to the vehicle to find his wife murdered."

The judge says, "Does the State have any objection to the video being played?"

James responds, "No objection, Your Honor."

Goodwin plays the video, which shows exactly what the witness just described. Once the playback is finished, Goodwin asks, "Paul, is this the same video you watched the next day after this happened?"

Walker responds, "Yes, it is."

Goodwin says, "Thank you, Paul." He turns to the judge. "Your Honor, I'd like to have this admitted into evidence. This is a copy of a police report and medical report in the death of Mary Bates. The report states she was killed by having her neck broken. And this report is a vehicle inventory report from the police, showing Mike Murphy having checked out a police cruiser and leaving the station about a half-hour before Mary Bates is killed. I have no more questions for this witness."

The judge accepts the evidence, then tells James it's his turn to redirect.

James gets up from his chair, comes over to the witness, and says, "Hello, Paul. I just have one question. Why didn't you give this disc to the police when you realized it was possible evidence in a crime?"

Walker responds, "I didn't have it anymore. I gave the disc to Mr. Bates before I realized it was evidence in a murder. Once I gave it to him, I just assumed he'd get the video to the police, since it was his wife who'd been killed."

James says, "Thank you, Paul. I have no more questions."

The judge tells Walker he can step down, then tells Goodwin he can call his next witness.

Goodwin says, "Your Honor, the defense calls Doctor Jeff Benson to the stand."

CHAPTER 29

DOCTOR JEFF BENSON TESTIFIES

Doctor Benson comes in from the back of the courtroom, approaches the witness stand, and is sworn in. He's a fairly short Caucasian male and appears to be quite a bit overweight and slightly balding. Goodwin gets up from his seat to approach the witness.

"Hello, Doctor Benson. Can you please state your full name and occupation for the Court?"

Benson says, "Doctor Jeffrey Benson, PhD psychology. I work for the Center for Psychological Services."

Goodwin asks, "And are you familiar with the defendant?"

Benson responds, "Yes, I've known Phillip Bates for many years."

Goodwin says, "And have you had a chance to interview him regarding this case?"

Benson responds, "Yes. I've spent several hours with him and conducted a thorough diagnosis of his condition."

Goodwin says, "OK, Doctor, can you tell us, in your professional opinion, what was going on in the defendant's mind, and was he able to control his actions in this incident?"

Benson responds, "It is my professional opinion that not only was the defendant unable to control his actions leading up to this, he was also not able to fully comprehend the difference between right and wrong."

The courtroom erupts in noise, as people are surprised by this. The judge calls for order before telling Goodwin to continue.

Goodwin says, "Can you elaborate on that a bit?"

Benson responds, "Yes. This defendant is unique in his situation from any other person I've ever known. Due to his vast wealth, he hasn't had the same kind of financial stress as most people. He has many employees working for him. He has a greater ability to make things happen and achieve his goals and get the things he wants because of his wealth. However, in this situation, his wealth and power became completely meaningless, which created a great deal of stress. In his mind, his wife was murdered in cold blood by the officer. No amount of money or power could ever bring her back. She was taken away from him by that officer. This sent him into a rage he could not control, knowing he would never see his wife again.

"This is very similar to another well-publicized case. The case of John Hinkley, Jr., who shot president Ronald Reagan. He plead not guilty by reason of insanity. He had a strong attraction to the actress Jodie Foster. She did not like the president. In his attempt to impress her, he lost all ability to determine right from wrong and would do anything to impress her. He planned and carried out an attack on the president, not because of anything related to the president or politics, but simply to try and impress a girl. He was found not guilty by reason of insanity. He suffered such delusional thinking that he was unable to see right from wrong.

In this case, the defendant was sent into a rage that prevented him from being able to control his own actions and see right versus wrong as a direct result of the murder of his wife at the hand of the same law enforcement he has spent so many years in support of."

Goodwin says, "Thank you, Doctor. Do you feel that the defendant is still suffering from this delusional thinking or is in any way a threat to society?"

Benson responds, "Absolutely not. The trigger that set the defendant off was the murder of his wife by the officer. The death of the officer returned the defendant to the reality of what he had done, which is why he didn't hurt anyone else and immediately turned himself in. This is a classic case of 'temporary insanity.' The defendant suffered temporary irrational, delusional, and insane thinking as a result of an action. His action in response helped restore that balance."

Goodwin says, "Thank you, Doctor. I have no further questions," then returns to his seat.

The judge looks at James and says, "Counselor, your turn."

James gets up, approaches the witness, and says, "Doctor Benson, can you please tell us, in your professional opinion, exactly what is the difference here between the defendant's temporary insanity and a man simply taking the law into his own hands and seeking revenge?"

Benson responds, "Yes, the difference is 'policeman at the elbow.'"

James says, "Excuse me? 'Policeman at the elbow?' Just what does that mean?"

Benson says, "'Policeman at the elbow' is one of many tests used to determine a condition called 'irresistible impulse.' The way it works is this: Irresistible impulse is a condition in which a person knows what he is doing is wrong but is unable to control his or her own actions. 'Policeman at the elbow' is one well-established method used to test this condition. This refers to the question of whether the defendant would still have committed the crime for which he is accused if he had a police officer standing right next to him when he committed it. Well, this case very clearly demonstrates that he would have because of one simple fact: The deceased person was himself a police officer in full uniform in a crowded restaurant. The defendant was filled with such rage during that moment that nothing was going to stop him. Once the officer was dead, the defendant no longer had that impulse and was able to return to reality, whereas most other cases of 'revenge' would not have a person committing the act if they had a police officer standing right next to them. In addition, the defendant is a man of means with, shall we say, 'many resources' at his disposal. The fact that the defendant did this himself further demonstrates the irresistible impulse he was suffering."

James says, "Thank you, Doctor. I have no further questions, Your Honor."

The judge says, "Thank you, Doctor. You may step down." As the doctor makes his way off the stand, the judge looks at Goodwin and says, "Is the defense ready to call their next witness?"

Goodwin responds, "Your Honor, the defense rests its case."

The judge responds, "Very well. We will break for today. Tomorrow, you will both give your summations. Court is dismissed."

* * *

That evening, Phillip is having dinner with Goodwin, and they're discussing the case.

Phillip says, "So, what's your feeling on this? Do you think the jury will acquit?"

Goodwin says, "I don't know if they'll acquit, but I guarantee there's no way that jury will find you guilty. We have a solid case here, and the jury will have sympathy for you after hearing that cop killed Mary the night before. That voicemail from her was very powerful. And James is either deliberately not going at you as hard as I would have expected or he might just not have been the right prosecutor for this case.

Phillip asks, "What do you mean?"

Goodwin says, "Well, he's missed a lot of opportunities to object. I just figured he would have objected to things more. I certainly would have. For instance, Brad didn't object at all to me playing that video from the pawn shop. If it had been me, I would have objected on several grounds. The video was dark and grainy, and it wasn't clear who was driving the first car. And second, I would have objected to the fact that the video wasn't analyzed by a professional and that video could have been made any time in the past, or even after you were arrested. Any date could have been programmed into that camera system to make it look like that night. We could have staged the whole thing. Obviously, we didn't, but I would have objected left and right, and he just didn't seem to be putting too much effort into winning his case."

Phillip says, "Well, I hope you're right. I'm certainly not going to complain about it."

Goodwin says, "Me either. We'll see how it turns out tomorrow." He glances at his watch. "I'm going to get going. I have to work on my summation for tomorrow. I'll see you in the morning, and we can go over it, okay?"

Phillip says, "Thank you, Paul. Really, thank you for all your help here. Whatever happens tomorrow, I'll always be grateful for the help you've given me here. I'll see you tomorrow."

CHAPTER 30

SUMMATION AND VERDICT

The next morning, Goodwin has arrived, and he and Phillip are discussing a new development that has just taken place.

Goodwin says, "Phillip, I'm not presenting my summation just yet. I'm going to try to re-open the case. The police chief, Dan Brady, was here early waiting for me this morning. He wanted to give me this."

Goodwin grabs a paper bag from the table, pulls out the contents, and says, "After your testimony, and the testimony of that kid from the pawn shop, the police executed a search warrant last night on Murphy's still-vacant house. His belongings apparently hadn't been cleared out yet because the house was going through probate. Well, they recovered this from the search."

Goodwin pulls Mary's necklace out from the paper bag and hands it to Phillip, who has a very surprised look on his face as Goodwin continues.

"I'm going to try and re-open the case and call Dan Brady to the stand to testify about this search warrant and what they found. This will be absolutely undeniable proof that Murphy killed Mary." Phillip is speechless and has a look in his eyes like he's about to cry while holding Mary's necklace.

* * *

Everyone in the courtroom is seated, and the trial resumes.

The judge asks both counselors if they're ready to present their summations.

James responds, "We're ready, Your Honor."

Goodwin then responds, "Your Honor, we are not ready at this time. We are requesting this case be re-opened for testimony from a witness that came to me this morning with new information critical to the defendant's case."

James objects, "Your Honor, I object. We have not been made aware of any new witness and have not had the chance to depose the witness. Furthermore, the defense rested its case yesterday."

The judge asks, "Who is this witness?"

Goodwin responds, "Your Honor, the witness is the chief of police for this city, Dan Brady. He approached me this morning with critical information regarding the victim, Mike Murphy."

Because the witness is the chief law enforcement officer for the city and summations had not yet begun, the judge decides to allow the testimony.

The judge says, "I'm going to allow the testimony. Objection overruled. The defense may proceed."

Goodwin says, "Your Honor, we call to the stand the chief of police, Dan Brady."

Dan comes in from the back of the courtroom to the witness stand and is sworn in. Goodwin begins his questioning.

"Could you please state your name and official title for the record?"

Brady responds, "Dan Brady. I'm the chief of police for this city."

Goodwin continues. "Ladies and gentlemen of the jury, based on the prior testimony given by the defendant, Phillip Bates, as well as the testimony given by the owner of the pawn shop, Paul Walker, the police department executed a search warrant on the home of officer Mike Murphy last night. Now Dan, could you please tell this court what the results of this search warrant were?"

Brady responds, "We found the necklace belonging to the wife of the defendant in the home of the deceased officer."

Noise erupts in the courtroom before the judge calls for order.

Goodwin grabs the bag with the necklace and paperwork related to the search warrant from his table. He pulls the necklace out of the bag and holds it up as he continues.

"Is this the necklace you're referring to?"

Brady responds, "Yes, that's the necklace we found."

Goodwin responds, "And this was found in the home of the victim, Officer Mike Murphy?"

Dan responds, "That's correct."

James says, "Your Honor, I object. We have no way of knowing whose necklace that is. For all we know, it could have belonged to a friend of the victim."

Goodwin responds, "Your Honor, this necklace is a very detailed necklace, with a large diamond on the end of it. Notice here that it also has a small piece of gold hear near the point where the ends of the necklace connect together. This piece of gold has an inscription on it."

He hands the necklace to Dan, asking him if he can read the inscription.

Dan responds, "To my love, Mary."

Several loud gasps are heard from the audience. Goodwin walks over to the board with photos and lifts up the pictures to a picture showing Mary Bates wearing the necklace. He then takes the necklace from Dan, walks over to the jury box, and holds it up closer for them to see it matches the necklace on the picture.

He continues, "This is the necklace. The inscription and picture, and location where it was found, make that clear."

The judge rules, "Objection overruled."

Goodwin takes the necklace over and hands it to Phillip, who has tears in his eyes as he takes it and just holds on to it. Goodwin continues.

"Your Honor, we have no further questions."

The judge says to James, "Does the prosecution wish to redirect?"

James stands up, approaches Brady, and says, "Chief Brady, why did you wait until last night to execute a warrant on the residence of this officer? Why wasn't this done immediately following his death?"

Dan responds, "We had no reason or grounds to execute a search warrant on the home of a victim. We execute a search warrant on a residence if the occupant is suspected of committing a crime. Mike Murphy was not a suspect in the murder of Mary Bates. He became a suspect based on the testimony of the defendant and the owner of the pawn shop on the night of her murder. Once he became a suspect, we had grounds to execute a search warrant at that time."

James responds, "Your Honor, I have no further questions."

The judge says, "You may step down, sir."

Brady leaves the witness stand.

The judge asks, "Are both the defense and prosecution now ready to give their summations?"

Both attorneys say they're ready. The judge tells James to proceed. He gets up from his desk and walks over to stand in front of the jury and face them.

"Ladies and gentlemen, we are a nation of laws. Laws that are meant to protect people." He walks over to the board, flips to a nice picture of Mike Murphy in uniform, and continues. "This man put his life on the line every single time he put that uniform on to enforce those laws. His sworn job was to protect and serve you people, but he can no longer do his job because of the defendant. He can no longer do his job because he went from this," he points to the picture, "to this," he flips to the page, showing Mike dead on the floor. "He ended up looking like this because of that man sitting right there." He points to Phillip. "That man decided to take the law into his own hands and killed a police officer in cold blood, in full view of several witnesses. He did this in full view of children, even, and after putting in considerable effort to plan this killing. These are not the kinds of actions of a man who then claims he had no way to control himself. His excuse is utterly ridiculous nonsense. This was clearly a case of the defendant taking the law into his own hands and seeking revenge. This should never be tolerated. I am asking you to send a message that this clearly is not allowed in our society.

Now, while we can certainly feel sorry for the death of his wife, that man did not have the right to take the law into his own hands. I want you to imagine what would happen to this country if we no longer had police and courts and law enforcement. Imagine the chaos and anarchy that would take place if people had the right to enforce the laws themselves in any way they saw fit. This country would rip itself apart in a matter of hours. It doesn't make any difference how rich a person is or what he does for people or how much he helps people. NOBODY has the right to ever take the law into their own hands. You have a very serious decision to make here today. Your choice should be very simple. You have to decide if a man who's admitted to doing that," he points to Mike's dead picture, "is the kind of man you want walking the streets and living in your community. And that's the only criteria you should be basing your decision on. Just imagine if that man had been your brother or father or son. Thank you."

James takes his seat. The judge asks if the defense is ready. Goodwin says he is, and the judge tells him to proceed. Goodwin gets up, walks over to the board with the picture of the dead officer, and switches back to the page showing Mary Bates. He then walks over to the jury.

"Ladies and gentlemen, the prosecution has said you have a choice to make, and he's absolutely right. You have to consider that if that woman was your wife or mother or daughter or sister and someone killed her in cold blood after robbing her, how would you react? That woman was the lifelong partner of the defendant. Officer Mike Murphy robbed and killed her in cold blood, and he did it after being allowed to remain working, despite numerous warnings given by the defendant to his supervisor, the chief of police. He did it after being allowed to remain working, despite being involved in numerous incidents of obvious excessive use of force. This officer should not have even been on the street.

"Now, you must understand that just because a person is charged with a crime, doesn't mean that person has to be convicted of that crime. Being charged and being convicted are completely different. Forget the fact that this person was a police officer for a minute. That only makes it worse for the State's case against the defendant. Consider if this person had killed your most loved one. Would you want to kill this person yourself? Would you want the person arrested, and if so, would you want him to be sentenced to life imprisonment or death? This officer was already under investigation for the murder of an innocent teenager. This officer had murdered, in cold blood, the defendant's wife the night before. Imagine this man breaking into your house the night before and murdering your child or spouse. What would you want? What would you do?

"This defendant has spent the last several years of his life doing everything he can to improve the lives of people just like you. As you're aware, he's currently building a college to offer free education to people here in the community. He provides thousands of jobs here in this city. You have to decide whether all his work and everything he's doing for this city for people like you come to a complete and permanent stop here today. If the defendant is locked up for the rest of his life in prison, he will no longer be able to provide the services or improvements to this city he's spent years providing. The decision you're about to make will affect thousands of lives for years to come.

This police officer was a very bad and racist person. It was just a matter of time before he would have killed someone else, just as he did Bubba Wilson and Mary Bates. It was just a matter of time before he might have actually killed one of your loved ones. The defendant has prevented that from ever happening. Police Officer Mike Murphy gunned down an innocent handicapped teenager and then murdered the defendant's wife in cold blood. This sent the defendant into an uncontrollable rage, as it would most people. The officer was a dangerous individual who needed to be stopped. My client took action and stopped that threat. Now you must take action to allow the defendant to continue doing exactly as he has been doing. Allow him to continue to build a college for us. Allow him to continue to provide thousands of jobs for us. Tell this man," he points to James, "that that man," he points to Phillip, "is EXACTLY the kind of person you want walking the streets and living in this community. I know you'll make the right decision. Thank you." He returns to the defense table and sits down.

The jury looks at Phillip, who has tears on his face and is looking down at the necklace.

The judge says, "This case is now in the hands of the jury, which will now retire for deliberations. Please remember that your decision must be unanimous and based only on the evidence presented here during this trial. Bailiff."

The bailiff says, "All rise. This way." He then escorts the jury out of the courtroom.

* * *

Later in a meeting room at the courthouse, Phillip and Goodwin wait while the jury deliberates. Phillip has Mary's necklace in his hand.

Goodwin says, "I'm sorry, Phillip. Sorry for your loss, and sorry you've had to go through this whole thing. It never should have happened."

Phillip says, "Paul, you have nothing to be sorry about. You've done excellent work here. And no matter what the outcome is, I'll always be grateful for your service."

The bailiff comes into the room and tells them the jury is coming back into the courtroom now. Phillip and Goodwin look at each other.

Phillip then asks, "Already? It's only been an hour!"

Goodwin says, "Hey, that's good news. Usually, a quick verdict is better for the defense. I'll tell you one more thing also: There's a lot of people outside supporting you. If they find you guilty, there's gonna be one hell of a goddamned riot starting outside."

* * *

The courtroom is packed. Robert, Brady, and Williams are all in the back of the room. The judge is seated on the bench, and the verdict is about to be read.

Phillip turns around from the table, looks back to Robert, and nods to him. Robert nods back to him. Phillip then turns to look at the jury and sees several of them staring at him.

The judge asks, "Ladies and gentlemen of the jury, have you reached a verdict?"

The jury foreman says, "We have, Your Honor."

The judge says, "The alternate jurors are hereby ordered dismissed."

After the bailiff takes the alternate jurors out of the courtroom, the judge says, "Will the defendant please rise and face the jury?"

As Phillip stands and faces the jury, the foreman hands the verdict to the bailiff, who takes it to the judge. Phillip is holding Mary's necklace, which he brought with him to court. Several people Phillip has helped or who have had problems with Murphy are in the courtroom, waiting to hear the verdict read. The crowd outside the courthouse has grown to several hundred of people, mostly in support of Phillip. They're all completely silent, eagerly awaiting the verdict.

The judge reads the verdict, then hands it back to the bailiff, who returns it to the foreman. The judge then nods to the foreman to read it aloud.

"In the case of the People versus Phillip Bates, on the charge of violation of code 187, capital murder in the first degree of Michael Murphy, we the jury find the defendant, Phillip Bates..." he pauses and looks at Phillip, "...NOT GUILTY."

The courtroom erupts in cheers. The crowd outside also erupts in cheers, as the verdict was being broadcast outside. Phillip smiles and hugs Goodwin.

The judge says, "The defendant is hereby ordered released. The jury is excused. This court is now adjourned."

Several members of the courtroom come up to Phillip to congratulate him on the verdict. He looks at the jurors, several of whom are smiling towards him. Despite the noise in the courtroom, he says, "Thank you" to them. While his words can't be heard, the jurors understand what he's saying to them.

* * *

Following the conclusion of the trial, Phillip's businesses all resume operating as normal, and construction of the Phillip Bates Community College resumes. After an internal investigation, Officer Brian Davis is terminated from his position as a law enforcement officer for lying under oath. Doctor Malcolm Harliss is arrested and charged with fraud for operating without a license and is awaiting trial. District Attorney Brad James loses his re-election bid, as voters express their fury at him for prosecuting Phillip Bates in the first place despite the fact that he was put in a position he never wanted to be in.

THE END